THE CLUE OF THE CURATE'S CUSHION

As a young man, Malcolm Noble served in the Portsmouth
Police, a chapter in his life that provides some background to
his crime fiction. *The Clue of the Curate's Cushion* is the
latest in his series of mystery novels that follow the characters
from the 1930s through to the 1960s. Press reviews have
emphasised the author's sense of place and atmosphere, his
strong characterisation and first rate storytelling.

Malcolm Noble lives in Market Harborough where he and
his wife run a bookshop.

BY THE SAME AUTHOR

A Mystery of Cross Women
The Case of the Dirty Verger
Timberdick's First Case
Liking Good Jazz
Piggy Tucker's Poison
The Parish of Frayed Ends

www.bookcabin.co.uk

MALCOLM NOBLE

The Clue of the
Curate's Cushion

Matador
5 Weir Road
Kibworth Beauchamp
Leicester LE8 0LQ, UK
Tel: (+44) 116 279 2299
Fax: (+44) 116 279 2277
Email: books@troubador.co.uk
Web: www.troubador.co.uk/matador

This is a work of fiction. All characters and events are imaginary
and any resemblance to actual characters and events is purely coincidental.

ISBN 978 1848763 029

British Library Cataloguing in Publication Data.
A catalogue record for this book is available from the British Library.

Typeset in 10.5pt Stempel Garamond by Troubador Publishing Ltd, Leicester, UK

Matador is an imprint of Troubador Publishing Ltd

Printed in Great Britain by the MPG Books Group, Bodmin and King's Lynn

PART ONE

THE TRICORN CODES

ONE

The Cockleshells Club

There's no trace of the Cockleshells Club. It lasted twelve days and CID's Dirty Squad knew nothing about it. When Ben Sharp's outfit pulled down the little school, in '72, they filled the cellar with rubble and concrete and some people say that Amy Bulpit and the Bloated Boy are still down there. But no-one knows for sure because a doctors' surgery stands on that corner now.

For two weeks in the freezing February of '66, Ma Shipley pretended to sell old clothes in the wooden hall of the disused school. She piled them untidily on trestle tables so that the long room looked like a jumble sale. A couple of neighbours came in on the first night but, "no-one would want this tat," said Ma and they went away again.

On the second Sunday – two nights before Cockleshells closed for the last time – a fresh-faced bobby poked his nose in and asked what Ma was doing so late.

"The needies always want something warm on a wintry night," she said. "We only charge a copper or two. It's all for charity, you see." Ma was wearing a pair of heavy-soled brogues that she'd found in a cardboard box and a grandmother's overcoat with a buttoned up bodice and large pockets that sat tightly on her hips. Recently, Ma had taken to wrapping her hair in a net, but not one that made her look like an old biddy. She fitted it low on the back of her head and she thought it gave her a continental look. When Ma looked in the mirror these days, she didn't see what other people saw.

"And the baby?"

"Baby's fine," Ma said and joggled the pram to show what a good nanny she was.

But the policeman wasn't sure about the set up. He couldn't see a kettle and the old woman had no biscuit tin at her feet to take the coppers in. Of course, Ma could have kept her makings in a back room but, no, it wasn't right at all. Anyone working in a cold hall at night would keep a cup of tea to hand. This woman wasn't expecting customers. 'Who's told you to be here?' he was about to ask, but Ma said, "Everything's fine," so he left her on her own and promised to look in later.

When the coast was clear, Ma stamped twice on the floor and, down below, Scottish Carter switched the cellar light back on. The bulb blew immediately and the sour-faced overseer spent some time seeking out a paraffin highways lamp which he stood between the three tables. But the lamp gave just a pool of orange light in the middle of the floor; everything else stayed grey. Carter had hung shower curtains around the walls to conceal seeping water. The fishpond pattern and the shells that he had glued to the table legs made the cellar look like a grotto in the half light.

He didn't know who owned the club. Two weeks ago, he had collected the keys and one hundred pounds from a dirty magazine shop and promised to keep watch for all the time that the girls were there. But he never did. Not all the time. Sometimes two or three girls worked here, but not tonight. The dirty blonde called Stacey All-Night had gone off with a porter from one of the cheap hotels, and Betty 'Slowly' Barnes hadn't shown up at all. That scruffy brass owed the Scotsman money and facing him out for a third evening would have trusted her luck too much. From day one he had been promised other girls, but they never appeared. Perhaps he should kid them that there would be a floor show or a band but, he thought, who wants this job anyway? It's lousy. A freezing night, no more drink and just Timbers with a virgin in the corner.

Carter poured port into a glass and drowned it with flat Schweppes.

The woman with Timberdick dithered when the tin tray came to their table; she hadn't ordered drinks. "It's all in the members' subs," recited Carter. "No-one gets cheated in here."

Timbers laid a hand on hers, stopping it shaking. "It's better if you leave something on the table for the drinks," she said kindly. "It all goes to charity, you see."

Carter didn't spare the cheap tart and her nervous housewife another look. He turned away, went up the cellar steps and left them to it.

Billie Elizabeth 'Timberdick' Woodcock always presented a funny face. Her protrudent eyes and beak-like nose were too big. She had no chin and her front teeth wanted to push themselves over her bottom lip. But the mouth was squashed and bunched up, giving the teeth little chance, so they left spiteful tiny sores where they had tried. One night in '63, when we were drunk, Ernie Berkeley and I had joked that Timberdick's head was like an orange at the bottom of a string bag. The weight of the others had pressed it out of shape and it had to fit as best it could. I have to say, Ernie Berkeley brings out the worst in me.

Timbers was curious about the frowsty mid-thirties woman who had paid money to sit with her. She was sure that Mrs Bulpit was her real name and that, if Timbers asked for her address, the woman wouldn't hide behind a false one. Would she hand over her Post Office Savings book? Timberdick had no thought of stealing from her but pouted as she weighed the question. No doubt, Mrs Bulpit was one of those brainy people who did things without thinking. She had a flustered look as if she had left her living room in a hurry and, now, couldn't believe that she was here. She hadn't dressed for going out. Her home made skirt with its grey pattern cut on the cross, and the cotton top which would have done very well as an old woman's vest, were clothes that she would wear when she chose a day indoors. She had brushed her hair vigorously but it kept no shape, she had put on pale lipstick but the feel of it bothered her and she couldn't make up her mind how to sit.

"Oh yes," she said, reaching again for her handbag. "Yes, of course." She had paid before coming down to the cellar and now she was anxious to press more money into Timberdick's hand.

"I don't do all night," Timbers explained.

She blinked heavily behind the National Health spectacles. She kept touching the plastic tortoise frames because they were ready to fall off whenever she looked at her lap. Which she did all the time. "You don't understand. I don't want us to kiss or anything of that sort."

"Of course, I understand, my darling. We'll sit here with our drinks for a minute or two. Then – what do you think? – we'll have a little dance and talk about how you'd like to spend our time together." Timbers sensed that the butterflies in Mrs Bulpit's stomach had turned to quarrelsome worms. Yet, her sunken brown eyes gave no hint that she wanted to run away. It was as if, after thinking about it for months, she had summoned the determination to spend some time with Timbers and now she was thankful that she had gotten in deep before she had chance to chicken out.

It's different with girls, Timbers thought; you need to take your time with them. Where blokes were cold blooded or nervous but always urgent, girls wanted to feel sure about the woman they were with. Like, testing a cushion before they sat on it.

Suddenly Timbers called out, "I've got you!" and the woman's face fell. (She knew what was coming.) "You were the girl on Criss-Cross Quiz."

"Oh, I wish I'd never written in." Her voice trembled. Part of her wanted to close her eyes and turn her face away but a stronger impulse was to let loose a salvo of feeling that she had bottled up for years. "It's the worst thing I ever did, going on that programme. My Ronald bought me a blouse that I should never have allowed, and the television people dolled me up with rouge that turned me pink. It didn't show on the tele but that's how I see myself whenever I think of it. Pink."

"I didn't think you looked odd." Timbers meant to be kind but she was in the firing line now.

"You never saw me," the woman accused. "You've seen people point me out, that's all."

But I do remember you, Timerdick thought. I was listening to *Wooden Heart* on the record player and I was sitting in an easy chair with varnished arms that were sticky. Because I'd spilt coffee and not wiped it up properly. And you came on the box and got a question wrong about our city. And I laughed at you and called you names. I remember licking my thumb and spreading it over your face on the screen. It was so funny.

"They made me look foolish," Mrs Bulpit was saying. "Ever since, I've hated going outdoors. I want to stay in for the rest of my life. I work in a quiet place; I'm always taking ten minute breaks under the stairs or in a broom cupboard." She was speaking rapidly, her eyes darting this way and that, as nervous as a tiny garden sparrow. "Going on tele is the same as never being able to close your curtains for the rest of your life. People are allowed to peer at you. They think they know you but they don't; they only know a *papier mache* puppet that was shoved to the front shelf for thirty minutes and that's who they think you are for always. I was always good at school. I could add up and read before any of the others and I could remember things so I always came top in the tests. Lots of people thought I was an awkward, lumbering girl with too many brains but I didn't mind if they called me stuff because I knew there were things I was good at. But going on tele — - well, it gives you no chance to show any other side of your make up. Everybody in the whole country has seen that you're plain-looking and goody-goody and you can't ever change their minds. There she is, people say, the girl from Criss-Cross Quiz. It was years ago but it's all they know me for, and even then it's false. You never watched that programme, not a girl like you. You're only saying what other people have told you."

Not for the first time, Timbers reflected on how ordinary people understood so little about a whore's life. The endless, lonely hours spent watching mundane TV shows were something that she had in common with this doleful-eyed stay-at-home. "I do reading," she found herself saying quietly, "and not just love stories," but Mrs Bulpit paid no attention.

Timbers reached for her little hand, its veins mauve with the cold. Mrs Bulpit hesitated, mumbling , "No, no, I came here because I thought you'd be good for me."

"Of course, I'll be good for you."

7

Mrs Bulpit stared at the ceiling and held back some tears. "What happens if someone from the club recognises me in town. I'd die. I just know I would."

Timberdick laughed. "There is only me and the Scots Carter. He won't be around long; he owes me too much money. Don't worry, this wreck of a clip-joint will close down inside a week."

Timbers knew that the Cockleshells was just one of those fly-by-night dives that appear like weeds on the city concrete and, unless they are dug up or poisoned, they wither and die for want of sustenance. Too few people come through the door. The drinks are dishonest, the floor show never starts and the sticks of sparse furniture look ready for the moonlight flit. Timbers had worked in so many. The Waiting Rooms on Hartley Street, the back of Widow McKinley's Curiosity Shop and the upstairs of an old barbershop where gents came in for a trim but disappeared through the beaded curtain and climbed the narrow, twisting staircase to meet the women. For the few nights that they lasted, these fly-by-night clubs allowed a girl to think that she had reached a higher row of squares on the snakes and ladders board. But the snakes were always there to get them.

"I hate working here," Timbers said loudly. "And I'd love to murder him."

"Heavens. You too."

The two women looked at each other but didn't say a word. It was as if a curtain had moved, no more than an inch, but neither would risk looking behind it.

The woman asked, "How can we dance? There's no music."

"We'll have to sing to ourselves. That'll be good, won't it?" Timbers checked her watch. Scottish Carter would allow them another forty minutes before he interrupted them. Then he'd want the woman to give up more money.

"I saw you in the rent office," Mrs Bulpit said. "You were helping the sweetshop lady get some money back."

"Yes, I remember. Why were you there?"

"I am a council cleaner. Really, I don't want to do anything else. People leave me alone. In the library mainly but I do the offices or anywhere they want me."

Yes, she was a woman that Timbers would always picture in smocks and pinnies.

"And when this trouble came up, I thought of you straightaway. I thought you'd be good for me but perhaps I made a mistake."

"No, you didn't. You didn't at all." Timbers took the drink from the little hand and, insistently, led poor Mrs Bulpit to the middle of the cellar floor. She put one arm around the woman's shoulder and they began to shuffle in circles, no broader than a tea table. The soles of their shoes – Timbers' stiletto high heels and Mrs Bulpit's Paisley flats, hardly stronger than household plimsolls – scuffed over the dusty concrete. Timbers tried a Matt Monro song but she couldn't hold the tune, so Mrs Bulpit took the lead. Very sweetly. Timbers pressed a hand to the small of the woman's back, pushing their tummies together. When the head of dry wiry hair dropped into the cradle of Timber's shoulder, Timbers lowered her hand from the woman's back to the seat of her skirt.

"Please, no." But it was weak and said with a smile. "It's just that anything like that will make me feel sick. I know, I can't help it."

"Your husband's the trouble, isn't he? Does he work for the council as well?"

"Ron's a policeman, but he's much more. He's spying for the Russians."

Timbers raised her eyes to heaven. Vicars and judges and untouchable princes, Timbers heard it all. Since Christmas, she had entertained a young man who insisted that he was the real voice behind a famous name in the hit parade, a pensioner with pebble spectacles who believed that he had climbed to the top of Everest in the Second World War, and two impoverished tellers who claimed that they should have been heirs – one to the Woolworth millions, the other to the English throne. Now, she was going to dance with the wife of a Russian spy. Oh Lordie, do-la-la-de-dum.

"How do you know that?" she asked patiently.

"I've heard him pass secrets to them over the phone and he receives secret orders. They hide them in the railway arches beneath two stones with orange chalk marks."

"I don't know what we can do," said Timberdick.

9

"We can't do anything about the spying but he said the police will prove that I killed him."

"Then you'd better not do it."

"It's too late to say that."

There might have been something beautiful in the scene. Two women, alike in height and figure, singing lightly to themselves as they sort of waltzed alone across the powdery floor, their skirts interrupting the throw of the amber light from the paraffin lamp. Even the cold, which Timbers had grumbled about all night, might have given the romance a ticklish touch. It teased the tips of their noses and fingers. The girls made a picture that a French painter could have caught with just a few hurried colours. But Timbers saw none of this; as she led the women through their pretend dance, she couldn't help thinking that she was on the edge of a calamity that she could do nothing about.

"Come on," she said, supporting Mrs Bulpit's elbow with her right hand. "Let's lie down on the couch for a few minutes, just you and me."

"Please, I'm not that sort of woman."

"Mrs Bulpit, you're in a cathouse. You've paid money to spend some time with me."

"No, you don't understand."

"Sit on the little put-me-up under the staircase while I fetch our drinks."

"I know I'm going to cry. Maybe, if you do just sit with me." Her face was red with embarrassment. "You must call me Amy."

She followed Timbers across the room, so closely that she almost caught her heels. "Go and sit down, dear," Timbers said as she collected the drinks from the table. But Amy Bulpit wouldn't.

Timbers could hear Ma closing the jumble sale, upstairs. She was ready to go home with the baby and would want Timbers to finish things in a few minutes.

"Amy, is your husband already dead?"

"They'll find him before long, the man with the football. He said they'd be able to prove it, but I didn't kill him."

"Have you seen him? Are you sure?"

10

"The man with the football?"

"No, your husband, dear."

"No, not tonight."

"But the footballer told you?"

"No, not him."

"Now, if you tell me where your husband is ..."

"Dear Ron ..."

"Yes, Ron. You tell me where he is and I'll go and check."

"In Cardrew Street, across from the TV Repairs. But I don't know if he's there. Maybe, he's not."

"I want you to sit on this couch and wait for me. You'll be on your own but it'll take me ten minutes to check, that's all. Here, take my coat to keep the cold off."

The little woman began to make herself comfortable. She placed the port and lemon on the dirty floor and wrapped Timber's old mac over her knees and her own coat round her shoulders. It was very cold in the Cockleshells Club.

Timbers said, as she moved to the staircase, "Don't worry, Amy. I'll come back and if anything's wrong, we'll decide what to do about it."

"I'll stay here. I'll wait for you. You will shut me in, won't you? Shut me in tight."

TWO

Orange Chalk Marks

Timberdick wasn't surprised that Ma Shipley and the baby had gone home. The dark and dusty hall was empty, cleared of the rummage and trestle tables. Although she expected Scottish Carter to be thereabouts, it was too cold to waste time looking for him. She bolted the staircase door from the outside ("Shut me in tight," she heard Mrs Bulpit cry again), then she banged closed the double doors of the old school and ran up the middle of the street. At once, she regretted leaving her coat in the cellar. She folded her arms beneath her breasts as she ran. That cuddle and the effort of keeping her high heels in place made her kick her feet to the sides with each stride.

Days later, a disgruntled Chief Super would be brought in to investigate two murders and the loneliness of the night would be something that our fresh-faced Constable would emphasise. The last two buses had been cancelled so where were all the boys and girls, stranded in the cold?

"Cold, was it?" the senior officer would ask.

"Freezing."

"Good Lord." By then, the Superintendent would have heard the stories of a young man tumbling, starkers, into the city's infirmary and of Timbers running through the dark without her pants on.

Being out late and running through the streets without enough clothes was one of Timbers' happy ideas. It was a little bit naughty and a little bit silly and a whole lot sexy. It was the sort of thing that the younger tarts, the stupid ones, did. She made her feet slap noisily on the pavements so that she could imagine little faces spying on her from the margins of upstairs curtains. The sound of her footsteps caught the rhythm of Wee Willie Winkie's nursery rhyme and, as she ran across the top of the street, she sang the first line in her head. Then she took up the vulgar version that one of the girls had taught her on her first night at Goodaldies Juntion, nearly twenty years ago.

She pretended that an old man, sitting in a fireside armchair with only a standard lamp to help him read, heard her running and came to his window to look. Recently, this widower – with grey at his temples, a flat tummy and arms as strong as a drayman's – had taken over most of her daydreams. She wanted him to make pictures of her in the flames of his sittingroom fire and when he was alone and undressed in bed, she wanted him to think of no-one but her, so much so that sometimes he couldn't sleep until three or four. Better still if he woke in the night with his head so full of her that he had to get up. She wanted him to live alone and only come out when he was sure he could avoid other people. She wanted him to be bothered by her all day. When he was washing up in his kitchen, he wondered if he'd catch a glimpse of her this afternoon. When he walked to the shops, he double backed or waited on a corner just in case he might see her. Sometimes, she made him watch her from the roofs of tall buildings. Once, he laid under a car, pretending to fix it but really wanting to look at her legs when she walked past. She wanted him to wear shirts with rolled up sleeves, listen to classical music, smoke a straight-stemmed pipe and know all about steamships (or church buildings). And if Timbers made sure that he never came to life, he could do all these things. That was so wonderful.

One man they called 'Popinjay', who lived with cats, did see her as he closed the curtains of his upstairs windows. "Typical girl," he said. "She can't run properly." It was unusual for him to be up this late, but so much had been going on that evening that he resolved not to go to bed until it was all over. During the past week, he had been suspicious of activities in the old schoolhouse. He had made notes of the comings and goings, the bits brought in and out, and the times when things were locked up and kept secret. He had constructed a theory but it was too fantastic to tell without proof so, tonight, he

13

had walked the streets. He called it observing on the stage rather than from the auditorium. He wanted to be in the picture. He had reported clues to the Constable (the facts but not his thoughts) but, honestly, the young officer was too wet behind the ears to take it all in. Even when Popinjay persuaded him to visit Ma Shipley's jumble sale, he came back and said nothing was wrong. He hinted that Popinjay shouldn't make a nuisance of himself. Now, as he pulled on his pyjamas, he remembered that he should have told the policeman about the girl. He had mentioned the man with the football and the black girl call Layna; they had been canoodling in a doorway. He had said that Ma Shipley had been in the schoolroom since half past ten, with Timberdick's baby, but he'd forgotten to report that Timberdick was downstairs. He made up his mind to correct the information in the morning; after breakfast and the papers, he could be at the police station before the proper Inspectors arrived for duty.

Past one o'clock in the morning and half way between Cockleshells and Cardrew Street, Timberdick Woodcock got cross about her scanty clothing. "Stupid bitch," she spat as she climbed the builder's fence, the cold biting wherever it could get. It would have been quicker to run through Goodladies Junction and turn into Cardrew Street where the Number 24 bus stops. But Timberdick preferred a more shadowy approach. If there was any truth in Mrs Bulpit's story, Timberdick didn't want to be seen on the main streets in the hours before the body was found. Gibbet's yard was safer. She was well known and several policemen in the city were ready for an excuse to arrest her. Carefully, she picked her way through the merchant's compound. Bricks, chunks of metal, cable and piping littered the way, but Timberdick trod steadily through them. The cold was getting to her bones now and she felt the moist air crisping on her cheeks.

A rich orange light glowed in the nightwatchman's cabin, close to the heavy gates that Timbers needed to open, but she knew the site was always empty after midnight. A man with his guard dog might turn up once or twice before morning. However, as she crept towards the wooden hut, gasps and cackles explained what was going on. Betty 'Slowly' Barnes, the most calamitous of Timberdick's friends, was entertaining the Bloated Boy, kept warm by an industrial burner with fierce naked flames. The flickering silhouettes of their figures made curious shapes for anyone looking through the windows. It was like a shadow theatre in the fairgrounds. The couple laughed as Slowly let his podgy hands run all over her stocky body and, when he tried to kiss her face, she made a joke of staving him off. Slowly was good with men. Once upon a time, Timbers had been even better. She had called herself 'the best little whore on Goodladies Road', although none of the others agreed with her. For a couple of years, when she was at her best, men used to come to Goodladies Road and ask where Timbers was standing tonight. She had known that she could make them pay four or five times what they meant to. She had never wanted to do it and had never enjoyed it; the first night on a street corner humiliated her and every time since had been worse. But she had always thought that she was good at it. Now, it seemed that all her regulars had grown old and died and not been replaced by eager young ones. She was tired of it all; she had been beaten by it. Just as Slowly and Black Layna would end up, one day soon. God, how Timbers would have liked to warm herself in front of that factory heater.

But she kept on going, out into Cardrew Street and along the wet pavement to the modest TV and Radio repair shop.

Wee Willie Winkle ran through the town
Upstairs and downstairs in her night gown.

'Across the road, close to the bins,' the Bulpit woman had said. Timbers searched the alley. Two dustbins stood at the entrance but there was no body. She even lifted the dustbin lids and reached a hand to the bottom, she even walked three times from one end of Cardrew Street to the other.

Knocking on the windows, shouting through the locks
Are all the children in their beds, it's past eight o'clock

Old Mrs Thurrocks, washing a long-haired dachshund on her

doorstep in the middle of the night, watched Timbers' search but said nothing until the skinny strumpet came up and asked, "What's happening, Mrs Tee?"

"Depends what you're looking for, my loves?"

"Anything amiss," said Timberdick, mocking the old woman's catch-phrase.

"Have you lost someone in the dustbin, Miss Timberdick, is that it? You wouldn't believe what people wrap in newspaper and throw into bins, these days. You want to know where Chip Fat is and you're hoping he's with the rubbish? He should be, the way he stinks. No, darling, keep still, Fritz. Have you ever seen a sausage dog like this one?"

Chip Fat was the owner of the fish shop, half a mile away. "I've seen enough of him, Mrs Tee."

She laughed. "Oh yeah, and what about him? He's had a bellyful of you, I bet, you old trollop."

"Don't, Mrs Tee."

"I know, my loves. I know. Well, there's nothing amiss for you around here tonight, 'cepting Boots and Hughes making a nuisance of themselves, playing footie against the side wall, but Boots is just out of prison so he needs some allowance, don't you think? Oh, we mustn't forget dripping Smee Ditchen and her new bloke. Been going hammer and tongs, they have, since eleven o'clock and everyone's heard them. Apart from that, nothing's happened in the street, I promise. Fritz and me, we've been walking up and down and resting and walking up and down again."

"No shouting in the alleyway?"

"It's been as quiet as the dead. Who are you worrying for, Timberdick? Are you missing Slowly? Because I haven't seen her on Goodladies Road for three evenings. Neither you, mind. Neither you."

"Night-night, Mrs Tee."

Mr Bulpit, the policeman, had not been murdered and dumped here, Timberdick decided. Neither had he been spying for the Russians. The story was all part of Amy Bulpit's worried imagination. Oh, Lordie do-di do-di da-dum dum. What were those words that went with Dixon of Dock Green's theme tune? Something about an ordinary copper? That was Constable Bulpit, she thought.

Then, as she turned towards Gibbet's gate, Smee Ditchen's live-in lover fell out of a front door and rolled into the gutter at Timbers' feet. Smee had cracked a china jardiniere over the back of his head and a trickle of blood reached down to the open neck of his shirt. He was cursing drunk and didn't try to stand until he had rolled up his sleeves for a fight. A row was the last thing Timbers wanted, so she turned her back on Cardrew Street and headed for the main road.

A bedroom window rattled open and Smee in her nightdress and curlers leaned out. "Don't you think of following that dirty tart!" she shouted. "Don't you bloody dare!"

"Aw, please let me in, Smee darling, Smee sweetheart."

The window dropped shut. When Timbers got to the junction, she looked over her shoulder and saw the spurned lover sulking on the doorstep. And, while she was turning around, almost tripping over her high heels, she noticed an orange arrow, chalked on the corner kerbstone. It pointed across the road where another arrow was marked on the pavement. This one pointed to the flint wall of the graveyard.

Timbers was half way across the road, when a stone was tossed across her path.

Boots and Hughes were leaning against the cemetery railings. They'd lost interest in the old leather football – it lay, discarded in a bank of nettles in the corner of the graveyard – and the boys were looking for other amusement.

"Billy Woodcock!"

It was so unusual for anyone in the neighbourhood to call her real name that it couldn't be heard as anything other than a challenge. A threat.

When Timbers stayed twenty feet off, the older youth stepped forward. "Timber-Dick!"

Again, her saucy nickname was hardly ever used in a coarse or rude way, but Boots Leonard had given it such an aggressive emphasis that Timbers knew she was in trouble.

Boots wore a biker's leather jacket with phoney fur glued to the inside of the collar. His denims were dirty and his pointed-toed shoes – comically out of date, even in '66 – were cracked and pitted. His sidekick, Matt Hughes, bobbed in his shadow; he smacked one fist into the palm of his other hand, but he was such an ineffectual figure that he looked as if he were trying to keep warm rather than promising violence.

"You owe me one, Billie Woodcock, being as this is my first night out of prison and being as you sent me there. Mattie, here, says you should give me a free go."

"It wasn't me," Timbers insisted.

Now she noticed a third strike of chalk on new mortar between two flints in the cemetery wall. She hadn't found PC Bulpit's body, but here were the footballers and the orange marks that the frightened housewife had babbled about. But Timbers couldn't look further. The boys were onto her. They began to walk around her, placing her in the centre of a circle. Hughes was the first to hit her, but it was no more than a shove, a light punch to her shoulder. Boots chucked a kick but she easily avoided it. Then, in a moment, Hughes had got behind her, pinioned her arms and dragged her back to the brick wall. She tried to wrench herself free but leaning against the solid brickwork gave Hughes more strength than he deserved. And if she kicked out, Boots would grab her legs and the battle would be lost. So, she relaxed, wanting them to think that they didn't have to try hard. Boots Leonard's sneering face came close to hers. Fag ash and stale vinegar clung to his breath. He didn't say anything but made her watch as he lit a cigarette. His meaning was clear; he was going to burn her.

"I bite," she warned.

He cocked his head to one side, trying to work out the significance of what she had said. Was this scrawny, worn-to-death tart really going to fight him?

"Make her learn," drooled Hughes, his mouth only an inch behind Timbers' ear. "Don't let her make a mug of you."

Slowly, Boots raised the cigarette to Timbers' eye level. He loved it all. The dark street. The violence in the air. His power over a nervy girl and the crawking adulation of his old schoolfriend. He wanted it to last. This was his best tasting scene in his own gangster movie.

Their eyes locked.

Timbers judged it right. As his hand muscles twitched, she snapped. He jerked backwards. She didn't get him but the surpise made him drop the cigarette.

Hughes shouted, "I've still got her."

Boots knelt to pick up the cigarette.

"I'll turn her to face you." But, doing so, Hughes twisted himself away from the wall. Timbers bunched up her knees so that he carried all her weight. He tried to release her but their arms were too tangled. They crumpled to the floor.

Boots laughed and kicked wildly at the mess of limbs. Before Timbers could get to her feet, his right hand snatched her wrist and lifted her to her knees. He was so strong that Timbers knew he could break her bones, just by squeezing. Boots knew it too. "I've got you," he whispered.

They stared at each other.

"Who's your favourite?"

"Please, Boots. It's you. It's you, isn't it?"

"Who's your favourite."

"Boots, I don't know. Boots, please don't."

"Yes, Boots. Do it," shouted Hughes.

"Shut up!"

"Go on. Show her she's got no chance."

"I like Steve Logan. Who's your favourite wrestler, Timberdick?"

"I suppose, Vic Faulkner," Timbers croaked.

"Ah, the Royal Brothers. Well, you've got no tag pal here, no-one to help you."

"It wasn't me," she repeated. "I didn't tell on you."

"Who did?"

She was thinking quickly. "Ma Shipley's girl. She's in prison now so you can't touch her. Look, if you want to take me, get rid of this oaf and I'll let you." She added, "You'll need to give me what's in your wallet."

19

He almost laughed: this woman, who was held fast and whom he was ready to beat up, wanted him to hand over his money?

"Do you want me to tell your friend what happened last time?" she teased.

His sneer turned nasty. His free hand reached forward, gripped her top lip between the thumb and forefinger and squeezed hard. Her face screwed up, her eyes squeezed and a child-like whimper strangled in the back of her beaky nose but, Timbers knew better than to resist. She'd won. She knew that Boots, in his head, had already given in and the viciousness of his pinch was his way of saving face. Timbers had to take it.

"Leave us, Mattie. I'll deal with this cow on her own."

"Don't make me go, Boots."

"Do as I say," said Boots, without taking his eyes off Timbers' face.

"I want to see what you do to her."

"Do as I say!"

"Bloody hell, Boots," whined Hughes as he trod reluctantly away. "We've been through it all. I've always been with you. Now you say I've got to get the hell out of it."

Timbers waited. She counted the little man's footsteps, counting them as they got quieter and waiting, like Boots, for them to disappear round the corner.

She wanted to plead but Boots gave her no chance. He lifted his hand, forcing her head backwards and making her go on tip-toes. Her hands flapped in the air, wanting to do something about the pain but knowing that they mustn't. Every bit of her wanted to burst – her ears, her eyes, her wee. Somehow she managed to plead, "No more, Boots."

"You're not fibbing, are you Timbers? It was Baz Shipley who told on me?"

Timbers made another noise.

He threw her aside.

She went down to her knees. She tried to cradle her mouth but it was too painful to touch. She could feel the top lip wanting to separate from the bottom as the blood congealed beneath the skin.

She said, through a mask of her fingers, "Give me what you've got in your wallet and I'll see you in the Cockleshells in ten minutes." She wiped her eyes.

"After what I've just done?" he asked incredulously.

"I want to get you on your own. I want something off you."

"If I pay up, you'll bugger off."

"I want to make sure you're not wasting my time, Boots. Not like last time." Already, it was difficult to form her words. Soon, they'd come out wrong. 'Like a bloody oak apple, it'll be,' she thought. 'Stuck under my nose, like Rudolf with a bloody growth, making me nod like a donkey at bloody Butlins.'

"You're a bastard, Boots. There was no need for this." She dabbed her little fingertip at the bruise, testing whether it was bleeding.

"Bloody loved it," he said.

"I want something off you."

"You'll get my money. We've already said that."

"I want something more."

A local taxi drove past, the driver raising a hand to acknowledge these two Goodladies characters. Timberdick the old tart, Boots the tearaway. Timbers thought that the cab slowed down and the driver watched their reflection in his rear-view mirror but she couldn't be sure.

"I want to set Ned up. I want him to sweat. I want him so jittery that he daren't come off the toilet."

"Not me, Timbers. I won't have a go at Ned-Mach. I owe him too much. God, what's he done to you?"

"Slowly Barnes, that's what he's done to me. And I want him to know that it's the biggest mistake of his life."

Boots sighed. "Go on, then. Get going."

Timbers had no chance to examine the orange chalk marks or check the graveyard for Ronald Bulpit's corpse.

The night Constable would say, two days later, that he passed the top of Cardrew Street at that moment and saw the ex-con handing money to one of the neighbourhood prostitutes. "I don't know which one, Serge, but it looked as if he was one of her regulars. They seemed to be on good terms. He tried to make a grab for her, down below, and she slapped his face but it all looked good natured. I saw her later, crossing the road by the old school hall. No Serge, she was on her own. Boots Leonard was nowhere to be seen."[1]

Beneath the cellar staircase, icy water dripped from an old brass tap but the lip wasn't in line with the drain so the water, for years, had soaked the floor. To solve the problem, Scottish Carter had propped a tin plate against the skirting; now the water bounced on the shiny surface and followed a channel to the open grate. The dripping noise was loud but Carter thought it added to the underwater atmosphere of the Cockleshells Club. In the night, when the place was empty, the drips were especially loud because there were no other noises. It was like a tinging second hand counting down the hours until dawn.

The bolt snapped back, the cellar door creaked and Timbers' two bony feet in high heels pressed down the top four steps. The weight made the tap move in its bracket, causing the water to change pitch for a few seconds until the footsteps carried on and the tap settled back in its housing.

The paraffin lamp still burned in the middle of the floor and Timberdick saw the patterns that their dancing had made in the dust. On one of the tables, a spent vodka bottle had been knocked over but it hadn't rolled off. Like a cold left-over from a game of spin the bottle, its neck pointed to the empty chairs where Mrs Bulpit and Timbers had sat.

At first, Timbers thought that the woman had gone home but the door had been bolted from the outside so how could she have got out?

"Mrs Bulpit, love?"

Why had Timbers called for her in a sing-song voice? Don't be frightened, she told herself.

---

[1] PC Newby's evidence was clear but lacked so much detail that it was ignored. Later, he was blamed for identifying Stacey All-Night, and not Timbers, as the girl at the junction but, thirty years later, he still insists the assertion was made by others, not him. "I always said I didn't know who the girl was."

"Are you there?" This time, she whispered so quietly that she could not have expected anyone to hear.

She stood still on the bottom step. Clearing her throat, she asked plainly and aloud, "Mrs Bulpit, are you here?" But there was no way out, so she must have been.

Timberdick had brought a hand to her throat and she couldn't stop blinking. Blinking with sore eyes. She held her breath and tried to step forward without a sound. As she crossed the floor, she realised that she was synchronising the noise of her stilettos with the tapping of the water on the tin sheet.

She reached for the bottle and pushed it into a twirl, round and round, the noise of its rubbing against the table top amplified through the glass chamber of the bottle. Timberdick didn't take her eyes of it until it wound down to a grudging halt. Then, her hand still at her throat, her face followed the direction of the bottle's neck.

The woman was lying on the couch beneath the stairs. Her face was in repose – her lips were together but relaxed, her eyes lightly closed, her forehead free of any frown. Her head rested to one side, her chin touching the shoulder of her right arm which reached for the floor, the pose of a woman who had turned over carelessly in her sleep. Mrs Bulpit was dead –Timbers had no doubt of that – but she looked as if she could be woken with a kiss.

But the peace on her face had nothing to do with the state of her body. Her dress had been dragged up to her breasts, exposing freckled plump legs, bent apart, and frumpish underwear. (Timbers noticed that the elastic had been repaired at the waistband of the woman's knickers.) The top of the dress had been ripped open so that her breasts could be yanked cruelly from their bra. They were out of shape and uneven – one pointed one way, the other was askew. They must have been mauled to achieve such a position. A dagger had been stuck in her belly and forced up under her ribs. The blood in the belly was still and sticky and turning deeper red. It had the look of something smelly.

The sleepy expression on Mrs Bulpit's face was so much at odds with the savagery of the abuse that Timberdick knew, without question, that the lady had been interfered with, horribly, after her death.

Timberdick wanted to touch her. Her hand reached for her white cheek but checked before it tested the soft skin. She stared at the knife and, before she could stop herself, she had dirtied her hands with blood from the handle. She gasped. She brought her fingers, blood seeping through their knuckles, up to her eyes. So close, that she could take in the scent of death. Timberdick screamed until her brains shook.

THREE

Peck Out My Eyes For What They Have Seen

Timberdick stumbled across the road, cutting her knees as she fell against the kerb and twisting her ankle when she recovered. Squawking with pain, she staggered backwards on the tarmac until she was caught in the headlights of a late night taxi. She squealed and went down on her bottom. The car slewed away from her, braking hard, and stopped when its front wheels hit the pavement. As the driver got out, fearing that he'd hit her, a dark cat ran from under the car and across Timbers' bare legs. She yelled and beat her fists on the road.

"Good God, Timbs!"

He collected her from the gutter, putting an arm around her skinny shoulders. She was panting; she knew no other way to hold back her sobs but the harsh night air made it worse. She felt the cold was squeezing her lungs until they cramped. She'd scraped her knees and grazed her bony bum and when she tried to get up, by first rolling onto her tummy, her knees hurt all the more. "Nooh," she drawled and started to cry. All the time, she was clutching her hand because the blood wouldn't stop coming; she didn't realise that she had gashed the seat of her thumb until the driver caught her wrist and held it high in the air.

"Lord, what have you been up to?" He picked her up in one go and Timbers was suddenly close to his swarthy face with its five o'clock shadow and the tacky smell of popular after-shave. He smelt as if he had just washed out his mouth in a dentist's chair.

25

"I'm all right," she kept saying.

"Timberdick. I can see. Someone's torn away your underwear, punched you in the mouth and stabbed you with a knife."

Timbers, who had learned in her childhood that it was easier to fib than explain, blamed the barbed wire fence of the builder's yard. "Something was going on in the watchman's shed and I wanted to see."

"Going on?" he laughed. "I should say so!"

"Please, it's nothing."

She was grateful for a familiar face. For twenty years Dave had been a local cabbie and a friend of the girls who worked on Goodladies Road. He recognised Timbers as one of the older girls so perhaps he looked out for her more than the others. He had often delivered lost gentlemen to her bit of pavement at the junction and, more than once, he had directed his headlights to frighten the wrong 'uns away. Yet, in all those years, they had hardly spoken more than a few words at a time so Timberdick knew little about him – did he have a family, where did he live, how did he manage from week to week? – but, on the night that Amy Bulpit died, Dave the Taxi Man was just the man she needed.

"Crike, the blood's pouring out of you." He pulled a scarf from his neck and wrapped it around the injured hand. "Get in the car. I'm taking you to the R.I."

"You mustn't."

"And then I'm calling the police."

"No, David. No. Not the police,"

"All right, no police. God knows what you've been up to, but if I don't get you to a medic, you'll bleed to death." He guided her to the passenger side of his old Ford Zephyr, opened the door and installed her in the front seat. "Just sit there and hold the scarf tight."

David talked all the time – the weather was good, traffic was light, business was poor, the city centre was empty –but Timbers didn't listen. For a few minutes, she withdrew into a dream-world of her own where cuts and bruises didn't hurt and the sounds of the traffic and lights from the street were nuisances in a real place that she didn't have to bother with, like the background noise to a nap. She dared not close her eyes – what horrors were waiting for her? – but she allowed them to rest on the car radio where Nancy Sinatra was singing *These Boots Were Made For Walking* on Luxembourg. In her head, Timbers hummed along to the familiar chorus, but she let no noise come out. She couldn't have counted the cars in which she had gazed, absently and resigned, at the amber lights behind the radio dials, keeping her song in her head as the men of different shapes and sounds tried to do to her what they couldn't really manage. The cars she had sat in had their different smells – they had their own dust – but they all had that stuffiness from phoney heat and the tacky footwells that made a girl damp between her toes. Frank Sinatra's little girl doesn't have to put up with that, she thought.

Timbers wouldn't allow herself to think of Amy Bulpit's body because her mind couldn't take the pictures. But she could put some facts into order. Scottish Carter and Ma had left the Cockleshells Club before her. She had locked Amy inside and had been away for twenty minutes, maybe half an hour. She had told Boots Leonard to meet her there and he had gone off before her. When Timbers returned to the club, the cellar door was still bolted from the outside and the place was empty. But what about the bottle on the table? Had it been there when she and Amy danced? Because she couldn't answer, the question became very important. She said it louder and louder, quicker and quicker in her head.

Then Mattie Hughes crossed in front of them at the London Road traffic lights and Dave said it was unusual to see him without Boots.

"He could be with Slowly," Timbers suggested quietly, hardly aware that she was speaking.

"Boots hasn't got her. She's doing all night with the Bloated Boy. She was with him at eleven and I saw them together, not five minutes before I nearly ran you over."

"He gives up good money, the Bloated Boy."

"He's a nice lad," Dave said. "Unbelievable, what's happened to him. Three years ago, he was a normal size and now, sometimes I see him and he can hardly walk. No ordinary girl will look at him."

Timbers was beginning to feel faint. She said again, "He pays good money," then tried to stop talking.

Dave took his eyes off the road. "Timbers, have you got your story ready? I don't want to know what you've been up to but the Popinjay was in that seat before you and he said he'd heard all sorts of murder going on in the old school hall."

"The Popinjay?"

"That what I call him. A fuddy old grandpa with cats. He wears a smoking cap with a purple tassel on top and a jacket that's got enough braid to make a bandmaster proud."

"I know him." She looked out of the window pretending to be unconcerned: nothing an old man said could be important. "So, Pop says there was murder going on, does he? Well, what he says is probably right. He knows most things. There isn't much that he misses." And he was a man who wouldn't keep quiet. He'd tell everyone what he'd heard in the schoolhouse. "But not while I was there, there wasn't. No murders at all," she said. Then: "I'm not going to talk any more, Dave."

The cold had got to her bones and, when Dave gave her a worried, sideways look, she realised that her jaw had begun to chatter. He slowed to a crawl as he entered the hospital grounds, ready for the drunk, the lost or the injured to blunder out from the verges. A quarrelling couple were staggering down the centre of the roadway. He pulled in until they were safely out of the way but before he could draw off, an ambulance blasted its road traffic horn and shot past them, its lights flickering with faults, its superstructure tottering unsteadily on its chassis. Dave leaned over his steering wheel and grumbled (his face was drawn and tired, the lines always ran deeper when he was struggling to stay awake), "Look at the state of their truck. It looks like a salvage job from World War One. How can we expect them to drive it safely?" But Timbers paid no attention. Once again, she had drawn that veil that gave her licence to ignore what others were doing. By now, she felt very cold indeed; the car's heater was no help at all.

At the hospital, he parked in a No Waiting bay and went for help. Timbers was alone for only a few moments but she felt herself edge towards panic. Her dreamboat came to mind. The widower in shirtsleeves was watching from the hospital roof, but she shook him out of her head. She couldn't have people spying on her tonight.

Are all the naughty girls in bed, it's past eight o'clock

And, never ending, the walking bass line of the Sinatra song thudded along the bed of her brain.

David came back with a nursing sister and two porters and when they opened her door, Timberdick went into a fit. She panted rapidly but, no matter how hard she worked, she couldn't suck enough air into her lungs. A spasm shot through the limbs on her right side; they crooked up into her body, a sort of cramp without aching. She couldn't straighten. Even when they lifted her into the wheelchair, her knee and elbow stayed fixed against her ribs. She could hear people clearly – "She's gone into shock," "Give her some air please," – and although she knew that she could have spoken, she hid in the comfort of her own world where she didn't have to answer questions. As they wheeled her along the corridor, the ceiling lights, blurred and sickening, passed overhead. In Timbers' mind they were the yellow lights of a passenger train crossing Rossington Street arches. She told herself that each coach represented one of the murdered bodies that she had found since coming to Goodladies Road. Friends, would-be lovers, people who never had chance to say sorry to her. Bodies that would never go away, they would burn with her soul forever. That was purgatory, wasn't it? How was she supposed to cope?

But she wouldn't admit to finding Amy Bulpit's body. Timberdick resolved not to talk about it, no matter how hard people pressed her. The corpse in the Cockleshells cellar would stay locked away.

Timbers was in a cubicle now. "You know what to do with this hand, Nurse Sims," the Sister was saying. "Get something right for a change, will you." Somewhere, they were telling Dave not to wait but he was determined to stay. He said he wouldn't leave until Timbers had come to her senses. Then, thankfully, she heard another casualty present an emergency and Timbers lay on her bed and hoped that she would be forgotten.

She made some decisions. She would stay in the hospital and never leave. If she didn't go back, she could be released from all those 'necessaries' that had dogged her life. Keeping going, that was the main 'necessary' – pretending, never regretting and always putting on a brave face. Well, she wouldn't go back to any of it. All these years, men had proved that she was unlovable. (And those who tried to get close to her just made things worse.) Good people went away and failed to keep in touch with her, even though they promised, the other girls grew up and moved on and now her own child couldn't forgive her. Well, that's all right now. Timbers knew, very clearly and very simply, that the one positive thing she could do about her life was to stay in hospital forever.

She lay with her head to one side and her knees tucked up to keep her tummy warm. She heard David bothering the nurses for information. "I won't leave without her and, no matter what you say, she's having a cup of cocoa before she goes. Haven't you got some Ovaltine or something?" He wouldn't listen to their arguments. "You can't make her leave until she's talking to people and making sense." When the Sister assured him that 'his girlfriend' was in safe hands, he barked, " I'm not going until she's talking, I said. Talking and making sense."

'Well,' thought Timberdick Woodcock, 'let's see how much he means it.' She decided she was never going to talk to anybody, ever again.

Then the safety barrier of screens shifted and Timbers recognised the face of a lady doctor who had treated her before. "I'm supposed to be helping an old man settle in the surgical ward, Timberdick, but they called me down to see you. God, look at the state of you. Come on, where did you get so many tears from? Come on, stop your crying."

Timbers listened. Her eyes didn't wander from the woman's face but she said nothing.

"Let's get you cleaned up. A fresh bright face, that's what we want, isn't it?" She produced some antiseptic lint, sat on the narrow bed and wiped Timbers' hands and cheeks. "No more crying, my Timberdick. Now, what about this hand? Dozy-Dotes! Who did this dressing? That young nurse with the ginger curls, was it? Well, she can do it again. Aren't you going to tell me about that lovely baby of yours?"

Timbers realised that the longer she kept quiet, the longer the friendly doctor would sit with her and the longer she could listen to her comforting sing-song voice with childish phrases. 'Dozy dotes!' Whoever said that these days?

"The cabbie who brought you in here – is it David? – he said that you've moved in with an old friend. Is that right? Mrs Shipley? Well, I was in the courthouse when her daughter was sent to prison. I had to sit with her for a few minutes, just as I'm sitting with you now. So, you see, I know Mrs Shipley a little, don't I? Shall I ask David to fetch her? I understand she can be quite strict with stubborn little madams."

A smile broke across Timberdick's face. "I want to stay here, Doctor Deborah."

"Yes, I think a few days with us might help. We could check you out from tip to toe, eh? We don't take enough care of you girls." She gave a playful smile. "I know what you're thinking."

"Yes, the last time you gave me a tip-to-toe, I ended up pregnant."

The doctor laughed. "I assure you, all that had started before I examined you. Now, do you promise to lie quietly while I get Nurse Sims to re-do your bandage?"

But little Nurse Sims was too confused by other tasks, so Timbers was left on the bed, listening to the noises of a hospital reception area. She thought it sounded more like a hotel kitchen – steam escaped, cutlery clattered, water gushed into sinks. Now that the doctor had promised to admit her, Timbers didn't need her no-talking strategy. A few days rest was all she needed, then she would be able to grapple on Goodladies Road again. But when David came to the cubicle and said that she was going to be discharged, the demons got hold of her throat again.

No, no, she shook.

"Easy there. I'll check. It's all right, Timbers."

Then a new commotion brought her to her feet.

31

Long-legged Boots Leonard was japing around the casualty department. He wore an army blanket draped over his shoulders but he had no clothes on except, true to his name, a pair of soldier's boots laced up to the ankles. His prancing legs, with knobbly knees, looked white, stringy and uncared for; they would have been better covered up. Although he needed both hands to keep the blanket from falling off, he flapped about, giving an unavoidable impression that Boots Leonard was trying to fly. His antics were as comic as a Jim Dale character in the *Carry Ons*, but Timberdick knew the strength in those gangly arms and tensed up shoulders.

"They'll capture me," he kept crying. "They'll peck out my eyes for what they've seen."

While others tried to catch him, throw him out, or calm him down, Timbers stood still, half shielded by the screen of curtains. She understood what had happened. Boots had arrived at the Cockleshells for their rendez-vous and stumbled across the bloody body. "He'll tell," she muttered to herself.

"Come on, love. Lay back on the bed." David had arrived at her shoulder, ready to protect her should Boots' attention turn on her.

"Get me away from here, David," she said. "Just carry me off somehow. To Ma's house."

"Was it Boots, Timbers? Did he rape you?"

"No-one's raped me, I promise." She added quietly, "That's to say, no-one tonight."

"What about poor Nurse Sims? What will Sister say if she loses her patient?"

Timbers pleaded. "Dave, Boots is going to get me into trouble. I need time to think."

Their escape from the Royal Infirmary is marked, with black crayon, in the annals of our City Constabulary as 'an undetected breach of the peace with suspicions of theft and criminal damage admitted to be groundless.' No-one could understand why Dave and Timbers didn't leave through the regular exits. After all, any patient could discharge themselves. Of course, the staff didn't know of her determination to avoid a confrontation with the Leonard boy; only David knew about that and he chose to ask no further questions. So they slipped away from the cubicle and through a pair of swing doors that took them out of the sight of the casualty area. They had escaped unseen, but they didn't know where they were or where to go next.

Forty-five minutes later, a desperate Nurse Sims, so sure that she was in trouble again for losing a patient, found two sheets knotted together and hanging from a window between the first and second floors. She reported that, when challenged, Timbers had become abusive. ('It was shocking, Matron. You wouldn't believe how shocking.') This prompted the phone call to the police.

But the sheets at the window had nothing to do with the fugitives. Dave and Timbers weren't even on the staircase. Keeping to the ground floor, they ran through the unlocked kitchens, across the refuse yard and, by the time tearful Nurse Sims was confessing that she hadn't confronted them after all, the taxi was approaching Goodladies Junction and Timbers was asking to be dropped at Ma Shipley's front door.

"Don't you think we should call Ned?" he asked. "I don't know what trouble you're in, but Ned has always been able to help you in the past."

"No! Never again! I've made that mistake before. If Ned knew half of what I've seen tonight, he'd have me arrested."

"Arrested for what, Timbers?"

"For some reason, I bet you. Treason, nudie swimming at parties — or nobbling horses. Yes, probably nobbling horses, he'd like that. He'll make anything up. I thought I could count on him when I needed him before but where was he? Sleeping with Betty 'Slowly' Barnes in Mablethorpe. He can't be trusted, David, and I never want to speak to him again."

"Weren't you supposed to be engaged last year?"

"He's dreaming if he's saying that. I never said I wanted to marry him. Never, ever."

"I don't understand. I thought you always worked together when things went wrong."

"Thought! Thought! You know what 'thought' did." She clenched her fists and rapped two sets of knuckles on her bony knees.

"I hate him. I shall never forgive him! I never, ever want to see him again, not ever!"

He steered through Goodladies Junction and pulled in at the old Hot Chestnut Archway. A Vauxhall Victor overtook them, the wrapped up occupants leaning forward to make the most of the heater. "See that lad over there?" Dave asked as the engine idled. "He was around earlier on. Watching. You could tell that he wasn't waiting for someone; he was just watching."

"He's the lad from the local paper," Timbers said as she got out of the car. She joked, "He's got freckles all the way down his back," although she'd never seen.

He put the taxi in gear. "Tell him to get to bed at nights. A lad like that can get into trouble if he's not careful."

"You tell him. Flash your lights at him and he'll sod off quick enough. Stace says he's a scaredy cat."

She knew that Dave would wait at the top of the street, wanting to be sure that she was safely indoors before he drove off, so Timbers straightaway pushed against the latch and stepped into the hall of the little terraced home. "I'm in, Ma," she shouted, although she didn't expect any reply. Then, "I've got to go out again. I won't be more than ten minutes. Then we'll have a fag in bed together, yeah?"

Ma called down, "Don't you want to kiss your daughter goodnight in her sleep?"

"I haven't got time."

"Any mother would, Timberdick Woodcock. Haven't you got two minutes for your own baby girl? I've never heard the like of it. I'll bugger you off one day. Then where'd you be?"

Timbers was sitting at the bottom of the stairs. "Don't be a cow, Ma."

"Be a cow?" The mattress complained as the old woman shifted her weight. "You say that to me! Me, who's taken both of you in. Knows me better than your own self, your baby does."

Timbers kept quiet and when Ma didn't speak again, she said, "Later," very quietly and left the house.

This time, the door to the Cockleshells cellar was open. As

Timberdick descended the staircase, she smelt the disinfectant. The walls were damp from buckets of soapy water and the rough paintwork had been scratched where scrubbing brushes had attacked every splinter and crevice. Mrs Bulpit's body had gone and her blood with it. Along with every piece of furniture, curtain, tin can, bottle, wax candle and paraffin lamp. The place was empty. It was as if no murder had been done here. At first, she was relieved because she could prolong her pretence that this awful thing hadn't happened. But then, she remembered Boots Leonard's alarm. 'They'll peck out my eyes for what they've seen.' A lonely fear turned her stomach. She wouldn't go to the police (because she couldn't stand going through it all in detail, because the detectives would make her head burst with questions, because she'd be their first suspect, because things had happened in the past, because of so many things so many times over). She would keep the murder secret and tell no-one, but Timbers knew that her silence wouldn't be enough. The people who had butchered Amy Bulpit wanted to kill her in the same horrible way.

FOUR

The Vicar's Locked Room Mystery

My interview with the police surgeon had gone well – he restricted me to light duties for another six months which I reckoned I could stretch until they pensioned me off – and my cursory two minutes with the Chief Constable indicated that his daughter was still speaking up for me. "Rowena says that your Police Dance Orchestra is a great success," he remarked. "Adcum Ops has recommended funds for next year and I expect to sign them off this week. Against some opposition, I have to say. Money is tight, Machray, what with the new HQ. Light duties shouldn't interrupt the woodwind and brass, hey? Perhaps we could involve the BBC." He tucked in the flap of my dossier. "Very well," he said, meaning, 'off you go,' but he called me back before I was through the door. "Have you read the report of the Superior Officer's Dinner Dance? That was some sort of ruckus, hey? Thank you for your efforts to keep order from the bandstand but, you understand, I do have to protect my own position. You understand that, don't you? The office of the Chief Constable."

I said that I did, though mainly I didn't. Still, I was feeling pretty chuffed as I plodded through the basement passages of Police Headquarters. Down here, the paint was dirty yellow. (No-one called it magnolia in those days.) The walls were decked with portraits of old favourites. Colonels, Directors General and one Police Sergeant Major. I wondered how dead celebrities feel when they are reduced from the foyers and corridors of power to dingy basement nooks. The old building felt like a ferrets club. (That's what my uncle called the exclusive parts of Military Intelligence.) Half the people walked around with smug expressions on their faces because they were 'in the know'. Others were only on the edge but they looked just as smug because they had landed cushy jobs. As a lot, I couldn't stomach them, but I'd heard that Herbert Jayne had been brought in from retirement so I made sure that I called into the library before I left.

"Catalogue the books, Mr Jayne, they said. Get them in order before we move to the new building next year. Turns out, they want me to throw half of them away. Reduce space, Mr Jayne, that's the order of the day." He worked in carpet slippers and a cardigan with holes at the elbows. He chain smoked cigarettes without filter tips, the kettle was never off and old books had been stacked into the shapes of a desk and two chairs. Herb had worked nights for most of his career and it showed. I looked at the mess of coloured pencils and slips of paper and I concluded that the index was progressing well.

"How's your Timberdick?" he asked.

"She's never been my Timberdick."

"Word was, you were getting married."

"She threw me over, Herb. Chucked me. She won't even talk to me now."

"No worse than you deserve."

"It was a misunderstanding."

"That's fine, then. We all misunderstood that you went off for a dirty weekend with a girl half your age."

"Herb, I'm fifty six. Half my age is ..."

"Half your age is unconventional, Mr Machray. Worse, it's still likely to frighten the horses. England swings, Ned, but you and I don't."

"It was a birthday surprise. Betty Barnes loves Cliff Richards so I took her to a fan club do, that's all. You know what these young rock and rollers are like."

"She provides a particular service, I hear."

"Well, that's nothing to do with me."

"She plays Night Nurse and Naughty Nephews."

"There is nothing in those stories," I insisted.

"Quite. They're all a misunderstanding." He pushed past me, disappeared behind a column of manila files and called: "You need to look out, Ned. There's an estate inspection going ahead. They want to reduce the Force leases by twenty per cent." He re-appeared with a gingham table cloth and paper plates. "It's all part of paying for the new Headquarters."

"They won't sell Shooter's Grove," I insisted.

"No. But they might move you out and someone else in."

I had been allocated Shooter's Grove three years ago. This large Victorian house used to be a Divisional Training School but no-one wanted it now so, although I was supposed to occupy only the bedsittingroom on the top floor, I pretty much had the run of the place. I enjoyed playing on the two staircases and in the two bathrooms (can you imagine this luxury?), but I couldn't get used to some parts of the building. The kitchen was extraordinarily large; it felt cold and empty and I had no hope of filling its pantry. I always thought that it was someone else's kitchen (which it was, of course).

And, although I had planted great green leaves over the front doorstep, people continued to post mail through the letterbox. Nevertheless, Herb's suggestion of impending disturbance was bad news. What about my model railways on the second floor? And where would my Police Dance Orchestra rehearse if Shooter's Grove was taken over?

"Lunch!" declared Herb, dragging a tea-chest of books to the middle of the floor and covering it with the chequered cloth.

"It's not half past eleven yet," I objected.

"Then we'll have to make it last," he said. He set out a picnic of cold chicken (purloined from the steward's store), cockles, pickled onions and cheese crackers. He saw my cautious look when he poured two beakers of beer, smuggled through reception in a Thermos flask. "It's no different from the Chief's cocktail cabinet. He says it's for entertaining. So's my Thermos. I'm entertaining you, aren't I?"

He provided a tea-cloth, which I tucked into the neck of my shirt. I decided to polish off the chicken before picking at the nibbles. Herb, who kept saying "Here, don't forget your beer," and "Don't let your ale get warm," regarded this treat as the main feature of his morning. When I asked for gossip, he wouldn't give any away, the first time, but as the business of eating drew to its end, he confided, "The knives are out for Adcum Ops. The top table are circling around like conspirators at the forum."

He knew this was more bad news for me because, although the Chief's daughter had got me into Shooter's Grove, it was Adcum Ops' patronage that kept me there.

"Old Ned needs to butter his parsnips."

(That referred to Rowena, the girl in question, I think. He wanted me to make sure that she kept me in mind.)

Someone knocked on the door and we both stayed quiet. A young woman spoke his name, tried the door handle and she swore, calling him old and useless, before she went away.

Herb leaned forward and whispered, "Ron Bulpit's run off with his wife." He wiped salt from his lips with the back of two fingers, then licked them.

"Don't be silly," I said. "You can't run off with your own wife. It's like striking on Christmas Day."

"Well, neither's been seen since Sunday. I had Personnel down here this morning, wanting a photograph of him. I gave them the run around, of course. 'Has his file gone missing?' I asked. 'It's one of the B to D blue tickets,' she said, meaning God-knows-what. 'Well, I might have a picture of his passing out parade if you've got the date.' So she trotted back upstairs for the date and when she came back I said it didn't matter. 'I've already checked and we haven't got them,' I said. I said, 'What about sports pictures. I think he might be interested in sport.' She said she wouldn't know without his file and I suggested that she should check with the social club. So she toddled off to ring them."

"I don't think I've ever met the wife," I remarked.

"No, she keeps herself to herself. She's not the sort to be found on her husband's arm at a dinner dance. There was a story in '59; it might be of interest." He reached down to his feet and found an old envelope. He took out a photograph and passed it to me. "That's her in the front row, watching Ron and his pals march past."

I chuckled. "So you had the picture all the time."

"I can't let them have our past, Ned. They'll burn it all, if we give them chance."

I noticed that the old man's eyes had filled with tears. I felt angry about the way that he was being treated. All right, we were the past generation. Some of us found a corner to hide in. Others stayed in the open and worked on the art of doing nothing. But others, like Herb, had cared enough about the job to hand over part of themselves. He wanted the Police Force to be good at its job, so he had come up with ideas, worked on them at home and when they turned out to be good, he said, 'Hey, I was only doing my job.' Now he was watching all those years shrivel to nothing. We both knew that nothing could be done about the decline. If he complained, they'd say he was just a grump from the old school. "It's time you went, Ned. I'll walk you to the front doors. I like people to see me up and about, once in the morning and again in the afternoon."

When we got to reception, he clutched my sleeve. "Do you know what happened to my old card index? Special Branch said it was the best intelligence on the south coast, do you know that? I've heard they've thrown it all away, all those years, Ned. All those years."

"I've got it," I told him. "The boss told me to destroy it when I was investigating the Yvonne Young murder, back in '63. But it's safe, Herb. Safe in Shooter's Grove."

"Keep it for me, Ned," he said as we shook hands on the concrete steps. "We can't let them throw everything away."

When I reached the railway station, short of breath and with only a few minutes to spare, two young Constables were showing their warrant cards and hoping to pass through the barrier without paying. I had known Curtis, the ticket inspector, for years. "You've plenty of time, Ned," he called as I pushed my fare beneath the booking office window. "Your train was seven minutes late through Sykes Junction. You've chance for a cuppa, if you want."

I approached him and he clipped my ticket. "Where did those oiks go?" I asked.

"Top end."

"Then I'll take the bottom," I said and he smiled as I dawdled down the platform. But I hardly had chance to collect a Nestles bar from the sixpenny machine when the four coach train rolled into the station. Floosie Rowena – grown-up and wordly-wise but still the Chief Constable's daughter – tumbled out of a carriage and into my arms.

"London's beastly," she declared. "I've had to carry this lot all through the Underground." She looked down as she re-arranged three paper carriers at her feet.

Curtis was already blowing his whistle. I climbed aboard and turned around to talk through the open window. "Rowena, are they going to throw me out of Shooter's Grove?"

"Oh, good God, Ned. Leave it alone, will you? I'll talk to Daddy. Everything will be all right."

The train started to move.

"Ned, Daddy says Timberdick's up to no good."

"I can't believe that," I laughed, waving goodbye. "She's an angel."

"But you must tell her ... " The rest of her words were lost in the noise of an opposing express train, rushing through.

"I'll tell her to be a good girl," I shouted as I waved from the door of the departing train.

"Tell her to keep away from Ops!" she shouted back. "Slowly, Ned! Is it true what they say about you and Slowly Barnes?"

Our Town Station should have been a twenty minutes train ride from County Headquarters but I could extend the journey by getting off, half way, at Cryer's Hatch and catching the later 3.57. This would allow me to spend an hour on one of my favourite platforms. But the Vicar of St Mary's spoiled the idea.

I was still waving goodbye to Floosie Rowena when he established himself in a window seat. He was a lean and streaky man with long fingers, big feet and deep lines across his forehead and down his cheeks and chin. He was never still and always looked on the point of saying 'Ah!' or 'See!'. He was a man who would have looked right in a second-hand frock coat and a top hat with its nap brushed the wrong way, like a disreputable Victorian Peeler. No, I decided, not a Peeler but the eccentric headmaster of a miserable prep school for boys who couldn't be placed anywhere better. He didn't stop talking. At first, it was leaking roofs and a cracked flying buttress, but I soon learned that the subject matter was unimportant; the Vicar could talk about anything. I don't think he took a breath in twenty minutes.

As the train tottered past Swingeing's Signal Box, he jumped to his feet and, gripping the luggage rail, stood at the carriage window. "I shall show you the very spot in a few moments," he said. "The actual spot, if our engine driver obliges by keeping to this slow speed. Exactly where I stood my easel and painted these fine downland meadows for three days last week. There, do you see? My, we've some of the best countryside, green and yellow watery meadows with their *Poa fluviatilis* and field bunting. Would you believe, a fisherman placed himself by that river on the second and third days, just in the right third of my picture. I couldn't have placed him better if I had designed the scene myself."

He sat down and, when I didn't speak, he carried on. "Is there talk? Come on, you'll have heard it. Is there gossip that the Reverend spends too much time painting watercolours in the countryside? How can he care for our parish when he spends so little time amongst us? Is that what people ask? People say that no-one knows the Goodladies Road better than you do, so you'll have heard any tittle-tattle."

I reminded him that tittle-tattle wasn't worth worrying about.

"You're a good policeman. I think you might be the very person to puzzle out a little problem that I have. A curious matter."

I stood up because the train was braking for Cryer's Hatch but he gripped my sleeve. "No, you can't go. I've yet to explain my Case of the Curate's Cushion."

I managed to put my head out of the window and waited for the station building to come into view. It was a corrugated iron structure with three different styles in its sixty foot roof. The windows had no glass, just metal plate shutters, and the doors had been adapted from a pair of sluice gates. The platform had an Edwardian streetlamp and a telephone hatch that had been in place before the Second World War. But there was nothing ramshackle about Cryer's Hatch.

Everything had been freshly painted with generous brush strokes from indulgent amateurs. A glorious wealth of flowers and hedges, including spots of modest topiary, dressed the station like a ballgown. A great hoarding – twenty-four feet long – had been diligently maintained, even though it promoted a discontinued brand of household soap. The line had been reduced to a single track, so one platform sufficed. Park benches had been mounted on the opposite embankment; they looked like a viewing gallery. Cryer's Hatch was that sort of railway station.

I said, "Please," but the Vicar wasn't going to let me go.

"It's a Locked Room Mystery," he said. "Just your cup of tea, I fancy. Surely you've read those detective stories where the deed is done in a room that no-one can get into or out of, so how could it have possibly happened?"

I could see the kissing gate to the station-master's garden, with its wrought iron decoration freshly painted. "I'm sorry. I'm afraid I'm not much of a detective and I was hoping to ..."

"Nonsense," he said, meaning that I couldn't have been hoping to do anything more important.

I wanted to explain that this was my chance to sketch the intricate gate mechanism that divided the country platform from the flower garden. The construction had been adapted from two cast iron benches with the Midland Counties wyvern crest on each face. No-one knew how the original seat had turned up at the Hatch because the nearest Midland Counties station had been over two hundred miles away. The gate was just the sort of curiosity that I wanted to feature in my lay-out so an hour at Cryer's Hatch, noting the details, would be time well spent.

"Actually ..."

"I know. I know," he said, still gripping my cuff. "But don't you think that we are all in too much of a hurry, these days?"

So I sat down and the train pulled away. "Come on, then," I said, failing to hide some disappointed resignation. "What's your Case of the Curate's Cushion?"

"I said, it's my little 'Locked Room Mystery'. Every Vicar's allowed one. I must talk about Valerie Bart, a thirteen year old girl, loved by her parents, loved by many people. She is the sort of girl who draws quite passionate friendships from her schoolfellows. Everyone will tell you that she's a good girl, first class. She delivers our parish magazine to the three roads behind the Royal Infirmary. Usually, she works this paper round on the first Tuesday of each month, but last Tuesday her parents took her to an orchestral concert, so Valerie promised to deliver the magazine during the lunch hour of the following day. I left the sackful of magazines on the floor of our old vestry and gave her the key."

"The only key?" I asked. The train was rattling towards the disused signal box now, another structure that I wanted to note in detail, one day.

"I have a second one, but it's always locked in my study safe. I've checked; it is there still and hasn't been disturbed. Now, as promised, she came to the vestry at twelve o'clock, unlocked the door from the churchyard and found the satchel of magazines, but she felt too tired to undertake the deliveries because of her late night. She decided to lie on the vestry couch for a few minutes. She locked herself in because she wanted to nap, but she found that she was too nervous of oversleeping so she merely rested with her eyes open, all the time. At a quarter to one, she started back to school, carefully locking the door behind her, but she quickly realised that she had left her purse under the cushion on the couch. She'd hidden it there for safe keeping during her rest. When she went back to the vestry, the purse was there but the cushion had gone. Now, it's of little consequence and she wasn't alarmed but the more she thought about it, the more it puzzled her. She came to me at teatime and we returned together to the vestry. Mrs Harold, our Wednesday cleaner, had rather spoiled things by entering the room from the inside of the church but she was in no doubt. The cushion was still missing. Now, if you can give me a simple explanation, PC Machray, I shall bother no more about it – because, I tell you, I can think of no explanation at all."

"You better describe the layout of the room. You're not talking about the main vestry, are you?"

"No, no. The old vestry was abandoned by the Victorians during the great embellishment of 1860. You may not have noticed it, round the back of the church. The exterior door is obscured by high brambles and the window was bricked up, years ago. I believe that the chimney is free, although no-one has lit a fire in the grate for a century, I should think."

"There must be a second door," I said. "You need access to the rest of the church."

He nodded. "Bolted on both sides. A curious arrangement instituted by my predecessor when there was talk of ghosts and creepy things."

"So who uses the room?"

"Nobody. I mean, nobody at all. It's a storeroom but a neglected one. I thought it was convenient for Valerie's purpose because I could give her a key without allowing access to the other parts of the building."

"And no-one else was in the churchyard?"

"No. Valerie thought she heard someone in the bushes but when she opened the door to check, no-one was there. The door was locked all the time she was inside."

As the train pulled into the next station, the Vicar got to his feet and brought his overcoat from the luggage rack. "I'm off before you," he said. "These puzzles are made to tease us, Ned, but please don't spend too long on it. I'm sure it's of no consequence." He opened the carriage door. "I can't love trains like you do. I'm always nervous of being left off or left on."

He had spoiled my afternoon but I couldn't help liking the chap. He offered a parting message from the platform. "I know you won't be able to get to sleep tonight. My little Locked Room Mystery will keep you awake."

FIVE

Outrage on Cardrew Street

I got back to Shooter's Grove in time for tea. I cut myself a plate of luncheon meat sandwiches. (I like to squash them so that the bread becomes pulpy and the butter and meat come together in a fatty paste.) I carried them, with a pot of Co-Op 99, through the jungle at the back of the house and sat down on a well-loved chair beneath a whithering cherry tree. I poured the tea and sipped it, and I nibbled at the corner of one crust. Then I balanced both on one knee and brought out a red tin box from beneath the chair. It had been designed to store milk bottles on doorsteps but I had a better use for it. It contained my 'books for the garden'. I put aside the Ladybird Books of Birds (Numbers 1, 2 and 3), the Observer's Book of Wild Flowers and a Collins Guide to British Mammals. I selected an old book with faded green cloth and a frayed spine, still in its brown paper bag. Just two days ago, a junk shop on Goodladies Road had sold me this bound volume of Model Railway News (1936), and I was sure that I'd turn up something relevant to my layout. But I had turned only a few pages when I admitted that the Vicar's Locked Room Mystery had been simmering in the back of my mind since that afternoon's train journey. I had to get rid of it. I found a weathered Biro in the long grass, got it working, and sketched St Mary's old vestry on the blank pages at the back of one of the nature books. I thought I had the shape and size of the room pretty well because I had spent so many hours in the churchyard at night. (Once, I had been assigned to spend all night there and arrest an expected burglar; he didn't show up and I went to bed for three days with a cold.) But I had only seen that part of the church from the outside. I marked the door near the corner of the longer exterior wall and the bricked up window. I guessed the location of the other door and scribbled 'bolted on both sides' against it. I was sure that the vestry didn't have a separate chimney pot so the flue must have been a convoluted channel that joined the main chimney somehow. That put the fireplace against the interior wall, next to the connecting door, and it also decided the most likely position of the fireplace. Finally, I printed 'locked before, during and after' over the outside door, then I put my head back and considered the problem.

I told myself that I had to approach each element in rational steps. First, I should ask myself if the cushion had really been stolen or simply mislaid. That seemed unlikely because the papergirl, the Vicar and the cleaner had searched individually and together. They wouldn't have missed it. Next, could the cushion have moved through some accident of nature? The wind? Or a bird flying down the chimney and carrying it off. I doubted if a bird would have the strength, but what about a cat? Now, I was getting somewhere. The chimney was the only available access and quite suitable for an agile animal. And, a cat would be attracted to a warm and comfortable cushion. Yes, the idea was something to consider.

I could hear the early evening trains pulling into the Harbour Station and the bicycle bells ringing as the factories turned out. Next door's mongrel had found two skinless sausages and had brought them to my back step before eating them. It was a peaceful tea-time but, I reminded myself, the evening would be chilly and I shouldn't stay too long in the garden.

I dropped off to sleep.

I came to at seven o'clock, frozen and damp. I had hoped to put in a couple of hours with my layout but now I couldn't face working on my knees on the second floor. The heating had been broken for a month up there (and a requisition for its repair would have prompted too many questions). I tried to settle in the bedsittingroom but, realising that nowhere above Shooter's Grove's ground level was warm that night, I resigned myself to sitting at the kitchen table with the Aga door open. That made me drowsy. So I stoked up the coke boiler, put on an extra vest and pair of socks and a jacket beneath my overcoat, then went out for a walk while Shooter's Grove warmed up.

The neighbourhood was gearing up for a busy evening. Amateur players were staging a Terence Rattigan drama in the local scout hut because their regular theatre had been flooded beyond ready repair. The Blue Coat Primary was open for a parents' evening, the old Methodist Hall had advertised a beetle drive and Bellamy Modes, a dress shop that had stood at the bottom of the Nore Road for years, was hosting a fashion show. Locals – that is to say, folk who lived within four hundred yards of Goodladies Junction – hurried along the pavements, laughing, chattering, clapping their hands to keep warm and bumping into one another in their happy-go-lucky way. Several recognised me and waved hello. Fat Mrs Savilles called out: she would be baking faggots in gravy with buttered bread later on, so I promised to drop into the Volunteer before closing time. A mocking cheer went up when ropy Smee Ditchen and her lover were caught kissing on a street corner. And when young Barry Holmes' record player was too loud in his bedroom, two grandmothers tried to out-do him with a raucous version of the Can-Can in the middle of the street, complete with dance steps that went too far.

But the evening also attracted visitors from other parts of the city. As I approached Goodladies Junction, the kerbs were crammed with parked cars. Husbands and wives, some with children already up late, were drifting towards the school and the makeshift theatre (they would want nothing to do with the beetle drive or Bellamy Modes). The grown-ups were wrapped in overcoats and scarves. The children wore duffle coats with toggles over woollens so thick that these poor pampered souls could hardly move their arms. They looked a sour and grumpy lot, doing something because they had to. At one stage, I felt that they were commandeering the pavements and I had no patience for that, so I squeezed through the cemetery fence and found somewhere to sit for twenty minutes.

I couldn't get rid of a suspicion that the Vicar's Locked Room Mystery had something to do with cats. There was no sense of proportion in the idea and I was annoyed that I was letting his bit of nonsense, this silly puzzle of no consequence, occupy me when I had much more important troubles to worry over. For example, eviction. And, if Adcum Ops was in trouble, a likely threat to my sick note. I smoked a pipe of Teggs' Russian Mixture and, when it had burned out, I sat tapping the mouthpiece against my front teeth.

A double-decker bus, on the wrong road, reversed into a side street, throwing its headlights' beam across the cemetery. I knocked the ash from my pipe and dawdled to the main gate. As I walked from the cemetery to the junction of Cardrew Street, I saw that a crowd, up-for-trouble, had gathered where Brown Gilbert was loading his truck.

When Clarke Pearson had been lost on the trawlers six months ago, little Josie went back to her parents and the newly weds' home was put through the salerooms. Brown Gilbert got most of the smalls and two or three pieces of the better furniture, including a walnut dresser that had come from Clarke's mum and dad in Cumbria. Now Gilbert and his young wife had turned up to collect their stock.

Nancy Gilbert was sitting on the back of the pick-up with her legs over the open tailgate and playing Clarke's Spanish guitar. Timbers, who was hiding from Chip Fat in Hot Chestnut Alley, expected neighbours to call – 'Shut up at this time of night'- but Nancy's singing was so easy that no-one interrupted. Couples in their bedrooms and kitchens, Art Ditchins doing something with bins in his back yard and old Mr Rivers sipping hot cocoa on his stairs listened contentedly and, if they had known the words, they would have joined in. Timbers had never realised that the second-hand dealer's wife could sing Country and Western so well; her voice had that rough, careless, hurting quality that matched the songs.

Timbers kept quiet at the alley's dead end, behind the concrete coal bunker with two dustbins in it. She was sure that she couldn't be seen because the truck was parked on the kerb of Goodladies Road and Gilbert was coming and going through the front door of the terraced house.

"Criminal," scowled old Ma Shipley, crossing from the Hoboken's back yard. "Doing it in the dark because you know

49

you're robbing a poor couple's home. Taking food from their larder, it's like."

"It's all bought and paid for," Gilbert insisted as he lifted another wash basket of unwrapped goods onto his truck. "And young Josie Pearson wants nothing more to do with the house, you know that. It wasn't a bankrupt's sale, Mrs Shipley, and everyone's sorry about what happened to Clarke."

"And what's the landlord say?"

"He says he'll let it before bonfire night," Nancy Gilbert replied.

"It'd do my Baz, very suitably," remarked the old woman. "A house like this and she'd be properly set up."

Gilbert said, "Word is, Ernie Berkeley owns the place." He went back into the house and Ma Shipley began to follow him.

"He never does!"

"He won it before the war," shouted Nancy.

Ma, half in and half out the house, twisted round to face her. "He never did!"

"He won it on the night Irish Dowell took her clothes off for money."

"And what would you know about it, madam?"

"I know a lot more than you think, Old Mother Shipley."

"Aye. And you've a wicked tongue."

I got within a dozen paces of Timbers' hiding place, when Ma Shipley barked at me, "She's not here, Mr Machray!"

I stopped in my tracks and turned around.

"I said, she's nowhere around here, do you hear me?"

This was nonsense. Timbers was in the alley and we both could see her. However, I backed away from the passage and met Ma in the middle of the road. "I don't know where she is and if I did I wouldn't tell you," she said. Then she started to plead. "Let her be, Ned. She's doing fine without you. The baby's fine and we're all fine together, on our own. She doesn't need you meddling, Ned. Please, don't go bothering her."

"Only, Dave the Taxi Man ..."

"I don't want to hear it. I don't care what our cabbie was saying. Telling tales on his fares, he ought to be ashamed."

Irritation burned on my face. I was fifty-six years old but these women were treating me like a lovesick teenager. I didn't want to chase Timberdick. I had heard, from the taxi driver, of her wretched night in the hospital and I wanted to check that she was all right (and, if I'm honest, to give her the chance to tell me what was bothering her). Mrs Shipley was determined to keep me away.

"Come on," she said, taking my elbow. "Walk with me, back to the junction, and we'll smoke in the Hoboken's dray yard."

But I shrugged her off. I had always thought that this old woman was a viper rather than a shepherd where Timbers was concerned. I expected her to be found guilty of some dreadful crime, one day. If you lifted a bucket of sludge from a Goodladies gutter, you would find Ma Shipley's toe print beneath it.

I stuck my fists in my trouser pockets, pushed out my bottom lip and trod away in a sulk. I wanted nothing more to do with the business in Clarke Pearson's house, or Madam Shipley, or Timberdick in the alley. I hoped that CID would find a reason to investigate the lot of them; they deserved one another. I was still grumbling when I walked past an old Ford Anglia, parked at the kerb. The streetlamp reflected on a head of light brown hair on the back seat. It was lying at a peculiar angle, I thought, so I stepped closer, rubbed the dirty window and peered through. Boots Leonard's neck was cricked and his top teeth were on show in the attitude of a man who snores loudly through his open mouth. Except that Boots couldn't snore because a carving knife had been stuck into his throat and he'd bled to death.

I quick marched back to the Pearson's house and caught Brown Gilbert as he was returning from his truck, empty handed. "Stop anyone going down this road," I ordered. "I'm going indoors to call the nick."

"No point in going in there," he said, his eyes peering into the darkness of the far end of the street, trying to guess what had happened. "The phone's been disconnected. Try across the road."

I knocked on Number 13 but got no response so I moved to Number 15. As an old man in pyjamas opened the door, a window rattled up at Number 13 and a pretty young woman poked her head out.

"I need to use a phone. I'm a policeman."

"Of course you're a policeman, Mr Machray. We all know that," said the old man. "I'm Smithers, East Lancs Air Dispatch, end of '43." He offered a hand, then diverted it to flick some mess from the shoulder of my jacket. "You'd better come into my place. You can never be sure of her up there."

From nowhere, a ten year old appeared at my shoulder. "I was looking at you, Mister," he said. "You've found an outrage, ain't you?"

"Off you go," I replied quietly, hardly looking at him.

"Not bloody likely. You'll have to give me a job or I'll make one up and I'll be one hell of a nuisance." He had his hands on his hips, one sock down and sticky golden syrup around his mouth. "I've seen what's in Mattie Hughes's car," he said. "And I don't like it."

"Right. Then your job is to keep everyone away, d'you hear? Not one soul goes near."

He saluted. Then, poking at a loose tooth and scratching the bare calf, he went about his duties.

"Leave the door open," I told Smithers as I marched into his house. Once in the passage, he thrust the telephone receiver in my hand and dialled the local control room. "It'll still be the late crew," he explained. "Nights don't start until ten."

"God knows where I'll find a Superior Officer," said the duty officer when I got through. I was standing in a narrow hallway. I tried to listen but the Smithers family tree was hanging on the wall above the telephone and I wanted to make sense of it. William de Loupe 'from whom was descended' was at the top. He had a wolf's head in a helmet next to him. So where did the Smithers come in? I went down one line and up another but couldn't see the name.

"I've no hope of Scenes of Crimes. They're all busy over Hessian's Yard," the voice was saying.

"What's going on?" I asked.

"God Ned, I said, they've found Ron Bulpit. He was stabbed with a chisel, they say. He's been dead some time, covered by sacks and slabs of old tarmac. We're not going to cope with murders in two places on the same night. Ned, you're going to have to manage until I can get someone over to you."

"His wife? What about his wife?"

Mr Smithers was in the kitchen but the door was open and he was listening to every word.

The Controller said, uneasily, "No sign of her."

I was still on the phone but shouted to the people in the street, "Get away from that car!" I could see that the lad had done such a good job of shouting 'Keep clear,' that a crowd had gathered to see what the trouble was.

"I said, get away from that car!"

"What's that?" shouted the Controller. "You've got a bomb in a car."

"Look, no. No bomb but I've got to go."

"So they've found Frosty Bulpit, have they?" asked Smithers, drying his hands on a teatowel as he emerged from the kitchen.

"Here, take this," I said and handed him the receiver. "Tell Control what's happened."

He was saying, "And his wife hasn't turned up yet?" as I walked into the street. "Can't say as I'm surprised. Amy Bulpit always was a strange woman, capable of dark depths, I've always thought. She had an affair, you know."

Ma Shipley was waiting on the doorstep. "Is it true? Ronnie Bulpit's been murdered?"

"Bloody traitor!" someone shouted. "We all know about him."

"Cut through his throat, Mr Mach," said Smee Dtichen, pushing herself to the front. "They found him in the cemetery ditch, so dead cold that his blood had turned blue. That's what they're saying."

"Bloody traitor! He and his wife, both."

Smithers came out of the house. "Force Control says that no-one's to go near the car," he shouted.

"Are we to clear the street?" a young mother called from the back of the crowd.

"No," I said firmly.

"Control says it's up to PC Machray," Smithers advised.

"Bugger Machray," said Ma Shipley. "We're getting everyone out." She turned her back and started waving her arms as she issued directions.

"Look, no," I pleaded. "There's no bomb, I promise."

But teams were already knocking on doors and calling people down from bedrooms. I soon realised that I could do nothing about the half dressed evacuees who began to spill onto the pavement. Mr and Mrs Tasker started to argue. The debunking was serious, she said; it could go on for hours. But he refused to let her go back into the house for sandwiches and a flask of hot tea. When she insisted, he grabbed the sleeve of her dressing gown and she toppled over, cutting her knees and one elbow.

"My God, she's cut herself," cried Smee Ditchen.

"First Aid!" hailed Mr Smithers, formerly of the East Lancashire Air Dispatch. "We need a First Aid Station."

Ma Shipley joined in. "Stuart Morrison! Set up a First Aid Post on the corner. Where is that Stuart Morrison?"

I was saying, "There's no bomb," to anyone who would listen but when Brown Gilbert asked if we should close Goodladies Junction, I said that I didn't care. "The whole farce is beyond me," I admitted. "Do what you want."

He nodded and strode purposefully along the pavement. "We've got to close the junction, Ned says! Ned says to close it!"

I felt like sitting on the kerb and hiding my head in my hands. Then Ma's voice said, "We've got a job for you, Machray. Two needies are hiding in the Tasker's back shed. They need bringing out." I gave her a deaf ear.

Cardrew Street was packed. People had flocked from surrounding streets to watch the evacuation. I kept low down with my hands wrapped around the back of my head. When I took a peep, I saw a row of pyajama legs under raincoats. One woman was still wet from her bath and another had brought a magazine to read while the children seemed to be having separate little parties, in twos and threes, on different patches of pavement. Self-appointed stewards mixed everything up by issuing instructions that got in the way of one another. It all had a wartime feel. I noticed the youth who worked for the local paper. He was using one hand to keep his specs on and the other to hold a torch over his notepad. The notepad was held by the lady from Number 13; she was scribbling as he dictated.

In the middle of the chaos, a motorcyclist was trying to tow a stranded car from the end of the street. "It's a classic American," he called out, waving his arms and wobbling. "I need to save it." But, above everything, Ma Shipley was bellowing, "We're clearing the junction!" and "Everybody out!" and "Empty all your houses!"

"Shippe, there is no bomb," I argued, quietly and patiently.

A lean and lopy character had turned up but I didn't recognise him. He looked like one of those elongated weasels on their hind legs that illustrators use in The Wind in the Willows. "You must be the PC," he said. I didn't catch his name but he wasn't from our lot.

We didn't talk to each other because an ambulance arrived and I busied myself helping the two medics load Ena Tasker onto a stretcher and the stretcher into the back of the vehicle. "Good show, Constable" he said. "Preparing a first aid post so promptly. A first class response."

"I ought to go with her," I said, climbing in. "I feel, sort of, responsible."

But a heavy hand pressed my shoulder. "Oh no, PC Machray. I need you at Divisional Headquarters."

An hour later, I had written a simple procedural statement which the elongated weasel read with a suspicious look on his face. Then he put me through an inquisition for ninety minutes with black coffee and no biscuits. He wanted to know everything I had seen or heard, or thought I had seen or heard, and what other people had seen or heard – or 'should have' in each of those cases. We were at the back of the building, high up, in the Xerox room. The machine had been fitted with an automatic fan that came to life every seven minutes, shaking the venetian blinds at the windows, then dying with a gurgling noise as if the whole contraption worked by water power. I wondered what we were doing up here – it had to be the coldest floor in the block and no-one else was about. But when we were interrupted by a second Superior Officer, this time from Special Branch, I realised two things; firstly, no part of this investigation was being handled by the local CID and, secondly, I was being kept out of the way.

"Ah, young Ned," said the new man.

I said in my head, 'Mr Machray. We don't know each other well enough for Ned and Gov.'

"You used to work for Buttermilk Dolby's outfit during the war."

Oh no, please. I didn't want to hear this.

"And now you report to poor old Adcum Ops. A good man, is he? A good Governor?"

"What happened to Ron Bulpit?" I asked.

"That worries you?"

"For God's sake, he was a policeman. Of course, I want to know what happened to him."

The detectives didn't want to believe my ignorance. When I kept on asking, the weasel clapped his hands to his sides and walked out of the room. Then the one in charge put his face close to mine. "Look, we know about Ron Bulpit. He took one chance too many. He knew the dangers. We'll catch his killer and deal with her. But this Boots Leonard, how does he fit into the picture?"

I said, "The crowd in Cardrew Street were calling the Bulpits bloody traitors."

"Ronald Bulpit certainly wasn't a traitor. He was employed on important intelligence work." He turned his back. "Who is the Bloated Boy?" he asked.

I wasn't going to let him interrogate me so I kept quiet while he fiddled with the window catch. Outside, 'Stand-by' Moreton, who had taken up his duties as a Detective Sergeant only three weeks ago, was trying to boil water on the corridor carpet but the kettle kept failing because of a loose wire in the plug. I pictured him on all fours, his ear to the kettle, as he waggled the lead and held it in place. Sergeant Moreton probably could have solved the mysteries of a plug's insides but he preferred not to try.

The investigator wanted to ease the tension between us. He sat down and laid his hands lightly on the desk top. "Ron Bulpit told your Governor that someone called the 'Bloated Boy' was running errands. We don't understand what he meant. Maybe, the errands were nothing to do with Bulpit's work, in which case, we're not interested. But I need to know who he is."

I nodded to the door. "You've got a new 'Defective' Sergeant out there," I said. (I knew that I was getting away with too much cheek; this man wasn't a regular policeman.)

"I've asked him and I'm waiting for his answer. Now I'm asking you."

I said, "David Harcourt's a young man who worked in the greengrocer's, three doors up from the picture-house. His mother died three years ago. I've not heard that he's got a father. Eighteen months ago, he started to put on weight, enormously so. Within a matter of weeks, he had to stop work. He couldn't lift, he couldn't bend. He could hardly walk in a straight line. But the family allowed him to keep his rooms above the shop. That's where you'll find him."

He was shaking his head. "He's not been seen since Sunday night."

"That's less than two days. It hardly matters."

"It's the two days when Ron Bulpit and Boots Leonard were murdered. I want you to find him."

"No," I insisted. "This is nothing to do with me. I don't know you. I've never met you, but I've met your type. You want me to do undercover and I won't. Not anymore. I've done my share of that in the war and afterwards. I've been tied to the under-bellies of lorries, I've clung to water pipes in cellars full of muck and I've almost died doing it. Tell Mr Dolby, tell anyone who's mentioned my name – I'm not working for them. " I stood up. "And, for the record, you employed the wrong officer. Bulpit wasn't your man. Herbert Jayne should have been on your team for anything to do with local intelligence."

Another detective appeared and leant against the door frame. "Jayne? Wasn't he the originator of the famous index. Is he still going? I mean, is the old sod still alive?"

"And kicking, I'd say. Alive and kicking."

I got home as daylight was breaking. I drank a beer on my back step, then I went upstairs and snipped the corner of a sachet of bubble bath that Betty 'Slowly' Barnes had bought me for Christmas. Ten minutes later, I was asleep in gritty suds and bathwater.

SIX

A Chief's Great Matter

At half past eight, the next morning, I was wearing an old white vest with stretched armholes and a pair of dungerees that I had last worn when painting the garage door. I had my boots on but they were undone. Stand-by, sitting at the other side of the kitchen table, disapproved of my scruffiness; after all, I was supposed to be on duty. He had watched me eat my double eggs, sausage (with brown sauce down its middle) and fried bread, and I was half way down my pint beaker of milky tea when he said, "I want you back in uniform, Ned. I need you to patrol the Goodladies Road like we used to do in the old days."

I thought, 'Please, don't tell me that no-one knows that place like I do.'

Before I could mention 'light duties', he promised that working for his new Superintendent would not change my sick note. "The Chief has brought in a foreigner, Ned. Our CID's been a mess for three years, you know that. He doesn't think that the local crew could cope with two murders at once, especially when a victim is one of our own."

Whenever I saw Stand-by Moreton, I thought of those precocious prefects at school who put their noses in the air, curled down the corners of their mouths and looked up and sideways at their masters. Like sanctimonious twerps. I wanted to belch, break wind and slop tea down my bib. Stand-by Moreton made me feel that way. I've never liked educated policemen, that's the truth, and

Stand-by was well schooled, if nothing else. I've always thought that clever chaps should become barristers or vicars. Really, an educated policeman has stolen a comfy job from someone who needs it.

"You're brainy, aren't you?"

"Oh, don't start this," he complained. "I paid attention at school and I worked hard for my Sergeant's exam. What's a fellow supposed to do?"

"What's a *Boa Fluviatilis*?"

That puzzled him. "I suppose, some sort of water snake. Is it important?"

"No. The Vicar mentioned it on a train and I didn't know what he was talking about."

"I'll find out for you. I've a friend who works in the City Libraries."

I asked about his wife.

"My wife?" he queried. "Why do you want to speak about my wife?"

"Because it was fine art, Stand-by, the way she pushed strawberry trifle into Lucy Dawson's face. It was the best moment of the dinner dance."

"Well, I don't see a need to mention it. I'll say this, Ned, she's very embarrassed about it and she has written – in her own handwriting – apologising to the important guests."

"She didn't say sorry to me," I said. "I was important. I was the Director of the Police Dance Orchestra that evening and, if you remember, I took a champagne bucket on the back of my skull. Doesn't that make me just a little bit important?"

He stuck out his lips and went, "We-ell."

(You always were a slimy squirt, Stand-by Moreton.)

"She wrote to Lucy Dawson?" I asked.

"Well, no. Things are still difficult between them."

"And me?"

"We-ell, she wanted to, but I said no. Look there's a history between us, Ned Machray, we both know that, but I'm prepared to look forward, to work together on this new case."

"Unless you count the dancing," I continued and hid my face

59

behind the pint beaker as Stand-by got cross. "We can't say that the trifle was the best bit if we include her dancing." I pictured her – we both did, I guess. She had hitched her slinky evening dress up, beyond her hips, and went bumping and grinding down the hotel corridor, pursued by a worried Welsh warrior from the Navy's shore patrol. "Tell me, Stand-by, why were you promoted to Sergeant, the first time? Was it your wife's dancing or your campaign against the dog owners of Goodladies Junction? You remember our old Superintendent? He told me that your approach to dog mess was revolutionary."

"Machray!" he snapped, toppling the chair as he stood to attention.

"Please, call me PC Machray. It'll remind me you're a Sergeant."

"If you insist on being offensive, I shall inform the new Super that you can't help us, that – that, that … you don't want to be part of his team!"

"Before you go," I said calmly. "Dave the Taxi Man saw Boots Leonard in the Royal Infirmary two nights ago. 'They'll get me for what I've seen,' he was shouting. Seems that they did, didn't they? And Herbert Jayne tells me that Mrs Bulpit hasn't been seen for three days. Tell 'Super' that she's your first suspect. Tell him, you thought of it."

He left before nine. I heard the postman at the letterbox but I took no notice. I locked the side gate and back door, then went upstairs to play trains for a couple of hours. Someone knocked at eleven but I didn't answer. When they called again, I still didn't answer but switched off the Hornby and went to bed for the rest of the day. Bugger the world.

Paul Tucker was desperate to make a name for himself that evening. He had been working at the paper for less than three months and, although he pretended to be a reporter, most people knew that he was only an office boy. ("A fetcher and carrier," he grumbled.) He needed one good story, that's all. He had got nowhere with the Cardrew Street fiasco. He had shown his three trypewritten pages to one of the regular journalists who'd taken it away and, later, Paul saw two of the old 'uns laughing over it. But he was determined. On Tuesday, the day after Boots Leonard's death, he bought a waistcoat and mac from Brown Gilbert's second-hand shop, and set out to spend the evening on Goodladies Road. His shirt collar was too big for his neck and the tie knot was screwed up and looked precarious. He was five feet four, he had sloping shoulders, broad flat feet and a chest that could hardly cope. He was nineteen. One eye was noticeably weaker than the other and he made little noises in his throat when he wasn't talking. As if a mouse was inside and wanted to get out. He had known that he was a peculiar case at school when even the most stormy teachers wouldn't shout at him for fear that he would buckle. He was grown up now but still the other chaps kept their swearing within bounds when little Paul Tucker was about. For as long as he could remember – certainly since he was four or five years old – Master Tucker had been building up to something and as each barren year passed by, he got more cross with himself.

"We know this place," the watchmaker said as he gave the boy a mug of beef tea, "and it's not a place for you, not at these times. Different for us. Our family has run this shop since before the war and my father always said that an old man should work where he can be seen. Regularly, for sixty years, Haraldsons have worked here until one in the morning and no harm has come to us. But you, go home, Master Paul. It is no place for you."

He took the lad to the window.

The road was wary and ashamed of itself; its people went slowly. A killer was on the loose. The murders of PC Bulpit and Boots Leonard sent chills down the dirty district of Goodladies Road. Nerves showed in different ways. The little grocery shops were empty by three o'clock, children weren't allowed out after school, stray cats – so good at sensing the twitchiness of a place – stayed on the rooftops and looked down. Smee Ditchen, leaving laundry at the Cardrew Street papershop, heard a message in the Guildhall chimes: 'Go home, stay home. Stay home, all night.' But there were people who had known Goodladies for too many years to stay indoors; they sought re-assurance in the company of others. The Hoboken Arms had a full house of regulars – they would go home in twos and threes

61

and those old men with knives in their pockets didn't talk about it. Young Haraldson (he was sixty-five if he was a day) observed from the window of his watch repair shop and saw people checking things – locked doors, inside lights, where people went.

The death of a bobby and a tearaway did not have the impact that, say, two dead girls' bodies would have had, but the folk of Goodladies were anxious; they couldn't escape the notion that the killings were something to do with them. This junction of three roads with its web of backstreets and alleyways was a grimy pocket of frayed ends and bad ideas in a city that, otherwise, had the colour, freshness and vitality of those years of the mid-sixties. Less than two miles from the Hoboken Arms people went about their business in a spritely way; they were curious, they were tickled by the notoriety, but the know-it-alls said that the beggars of Goodladies Road got what they deserved.

Without realising it, the old man began to repeat the family history. "There's been a shop here for more than sixty years. My father started it in 1906 and worked it until '45, when he was sixty-six years old and I took over. I don't see my son following me – fools' work, he says – but I've got hopes for my sweet grand-daughter. She's just fourteen. She's supposed to be helping me here tonight, that's what her parents think. But I know she's somewhere safe. Not out there. You don't want to go out there."

But the working girls had no choice. Timberdick had been out and about all day. She had dallied in the little shops on Goodladies Road, she had taken cups of tea in the cafes and snack bars and she chattered on the pavement edges. At dinner time, she met Ma Shipley with the baby for fish and chips. Timberdick promised to be indoors for her daughter's bedtime but, as the afternoon wore on, the promise grew less and less likely to be kept. Ernie 'Soapy' Berkeley, a whiskery-faced layabout with grubby cuffs and a worn collar, kept her in the Methodist Hall for an hour and a half. He insisted that he had no money to pay for his soup and he took several fags off her, but Timbers was patient; she knew that none of the other girls would spend time with the dirty toad. While he was in the gents, for the third time, she left two cigarettes on the table for him and hurried out of the hall. A church rang four-thirty as she trotted along Rossington Street. A voice from a sheltered doorway barked, "Are you working, love?" and Timbers sauntered on, without turning her head. At Queen Street she argued with a bus conductor who insisted that an old woman, unable to pay her fare, should leave the bus. The driver left his cab and walked round to support his crew.

"Leave her alone," Timbers shouted, as the pensioner purposefully wedged her whicker shopping basket between a seat and the luggage hold.

"What's it got to do with you!" said the man in charge. "You're not even on this bus!"

"Leave her alone!"

"She's got to pay!" The passengers in the lower deck cheered him, sure the woman shouldn't get a free ride.

"Old people should travel for nothing," Timbers said. "It's public transport isn't it?"

"Don't be ridiculous. I've never heard of anything so ridiculous. What do you people think? Ridiculous isn't it?" And everyone cheered again. "Now, my dear, you get off the bus and you, you old tart, bugger off out of it."

From there, Timbers crossed the road, aware that two young lads had stopped to look at her bare legs in a very short skirt, and she ordered a plastic cuppa from the tea stop. "Are you causing ramifications again, our Timbers?" asked the man behind the caravan counter.

"A bit mean with the sugar, aren't you? Here, give us the bowl."

Then, when the shops were closing on Goodladies Road, Timbers had gone to the back door of the chip shop and begged seven pounds off the fat fishmonger. He made her promise to come back at midnight, when his wife would be asleep, but they both knew that she wouldn't and they'd row about it before the weekend.

She had done well. She had thirty five quid folded in her bra but she wasn't taking it home. She'd worked hard for it. She had thought hard, choosing the blokes that she knew would pay well. And Ma Shipley could bugger off if she thought it was all going in the family kitty.

Instead, Timbers was hurrying to a horrible place, a knot – a crinkle – in the town's landscape, where so many bad things had happened to her. She had found a murder here, in 1947; she had been molested on the path and she had heard the horrible truth about her father. She always said that these things were old business, done with, but they never were. Strangely, she was drawn back to the place when she wanted its wickedness to protect her. It was as if she recognised that only bad fairies would work their magic on her behalf. Good fairies wouldn't want to care for her. And the run-down cottage of the dead Dirty Verger was full of bad fairies.

He had been dead for twelve years. The old railwayman's cottage had been boarded up in a ramshackle way. The makeshift shutters – not one matching another – were protected by webs of chicken wire, secured by nails that had been hammered into the frames and bent over to make hooks. (It hadn't been done by proper workmen.)

Even now, she was sure that she could hear the queer brother and sister singing their old fashioned hymns in the front room, though no-one had lived here for years. Timbers sang aloud, to keep the fairies from her head:

"Knocking on the windows, calling through the locks.
Are all the children in the beds, it's past eight o'clock."

She opened the shed door with a bang and a clatter. The same messy mattress lay on the floor. The old lavatory, cracked and filthy, still stood in the corner.

Behind the door, she dug and clutched at a loose floorboard. It lifted for her and Timbers reached down for the wooden trinket casket. Hurriedly, she married twenty of her thirty-five pounds to the savings that she had already stowed away. Then she put everything back and got out as quickly as she could.

Half an hour later, Smee Ditchen saw Timbers punching and kicking two lads in Kershaw's Passage; at one stage, they had her pinned against the wooden fence but she jabbed one in the eye and beat the other off with vicious obscenities. Just twenty minutes later, Timbers was back in Rossington Street – where the bloke had shouted 'Are you working, love?' four hours before. She waited at the top of the alley, next to the coal bunkers. She put herself in the shadows but stepped forward when passing cars could light up her legs. At last, he appeared on the pavement but, after she had taken his money, she said that he had taken so long coming that she could only let him have a couple of minutes jiggery-pokery. She'd make it up to him next time, she promised. Only three years ago, Timberdick had boasted that she could make men pay three or four times what they meant to. Now, as she emerged onto Goodaldies Road, and turned towards Stacey's pitch, she knew that she got through by cheating and lying; it was almost stealing.

Murder or no murder, Black Layna Martins and Stacey All-Night and the others had to stand in the doorways and on the street corners. Their customers, who came on their own after dark, felt safe enough in their cars, but the girls looked after themselves. Betty 'Slowly' Barnes hadn't worked for three days but Ma Shipley had been to her house so the girls knew that she was all right.

"She's busy with something," said Layna, the best looking of all the girls.

"With something," Stacey echoed through her dirty fingertips as she dragged hard on a Park Drive.

The women were leaning against the corner wall of the PDSA Clinic, an end of terrace house with blue signs, and blinds at the windows instead of curtains. Stacey's feet were over a drain hole and she kept bobbing up and down as she trod on the concrete surround. "Yes," said Layna. "I could tell that Ma wants us to keep out of Slowly's way. She's doing something."

"Doing something," said Stacey. "Out of the way."

"She's all right, though. I'm sure of it."

"Right though." Then Stacey saw Timbers walking up from Old Chestnut Alley. "Here's that bloody Timberdick. She gets right up my arse. I can't stand her."

Layna nodded, thinking of mentioning that Stacey hadn't passed the cigarette packet over. "God help that kid of hers. She'll grow up thinking that old Ma Shipley's her mother and Timbs is no more than a live-in lover."

"Yeah, a live-in." Stacey pinched the stub of her cigarette, took one last suck, then threw it down the drain. "I saw her with Ernie Berkeley earlier on. She said she'd promised to be back home to spend time with her nipper before bed, but I bet she weren't."

An old A35, a crock, pulled into the kerb and Stacey stepped forward and bent down to speak through the open window. Then she went back to the wall and Layna, with no real talking, got her long, stately body into the little car and the bloke drove off.

Bugger it, thought Stacey, now she'd have to stand on this street corner with Timber-bloody-dick.

A few moments later, Timbers stopped at the kerb. She saw Stace, talking terms with a well dressed boy, wet behind the ears. Timbers knew that she shouldn't interrupt them and looked to cross to the other side of the junction. Then a grey Bentley purred alongside; Timbers giggled and, as she trotted around the front of the car, the passenger door clicked open.

Timbers bounced into the large elephant grey seat and settled with her arms loosely at her sides and her knees comfortably apart. It all emphasised her availability, she thought.

"I thought we'd park up on the hill," he said.

"Lovely," she replied. The Assistant Chief Constable was one of her most generous boyfriends and he asked so little of her. As the posh motorcar progressed slowly through the junction and past the lights of London Road, Timbers was sure that she was in for a successful evening (although she'd be too late home for Li'l Timms).

"I'll feel better once we're out of the town," he continued.

"Just lovely."

As they passed the raincoated queue for the first house of *Krakatoa*, Timbers looked the other way; she didn't want to be recognised with a senior policeman. Nowhere was open, but yellow and orange lights spilled onto the pavements from the shop fronts. Curry's and Weston's were advertising new television sets and a husband and wife were rearranging the window display of their shoe shop. The Assistant Chief slowed down as a scurry of young women ran in front of the car to catch a double-decker that was already pulling away. Timbers thought that a young Constable saluted as they passed Trent House but Adcum Ops never allowed his eyes to wander from the long nose of the car. His face was worried – and the changing colours from the streetlights made him look mysterious. Once, when a reflection of purples and dark blues fixed itself across his deep set eyes, Timbers thought that he looked like a —- no, not a murderer and no, not a lunatic. Timbers had to ferret around in her head before she got properly hold of what she meant: he looked like a man on the edge of being sick with worry.

Timbers had sat in this sumptuous car several times and although she had been paid generously for her time, the senior policeman had yet to touch her, or show her any personal attention at all. I have always described Adcum Ops as the sort of fellow who went for bicycle rides in the Edwardian era. Timbers thought he was stony-faced, buttoned-up and chilly. Certainly he gave away little of himself. Timbers gathered that his marriage was difficult and that he struggled to have any relationship with his grown-up children, but Timbers had picked up no idea that her company was meant to compensate for those shortfalls. Not even in the slightest way. He talked but more often he was quiet. Once, they had sat in his car, parked on the quay with nothing to look at but a dirty freighter's backside, and Adcum Ops hadn't uttered a word for fifty minutes. 'He's an unusual one,' Timbers thought. 'But he's not peculiar, thank God.' She had suffered her fill of peculiar men. As the policeman drove out of the city and began to steer up the hillside, where courting couples go, Timbers was fascinated by the stern, tough face that couldn't comfortably wear emotion. She would never have admitted that she was attracted to him, but her curiosity was so powerful that it fell not far short of that.

They sat, smoking and watching the lights of the city laid out before them, both thinking, 'Why have we come up here?' Adcum's cigar burned slowly and he pulled on it only occasionally. Here's a man who takes what he needs but nothing more, she thought. Not like me, greedy bitch, and she sucked three or four times on her fag. Then Timbers took hold of his chin and kissed his mouth. It was a stony kiss, for he didn't respond and, although Timbers kept going longer than she needed, she didn't mean it to lead to any intimacy.

"That's a big thank you," she whispered when she drew back. "But for you, I'd be shackled to Ned Machray and, d'you know, I can't think of anything worse."

"You were cross at the time," he said.

"Too right, I was. You said that we couldn't marry because he was a policeman and I was a whore. Too right I was cross. But, I see now."

He said, "You should spend more time with the baby and less on the streets. A girl can't work the same way when she's forty as when she's twenty."

"Has Shippe been talking to you?"

"No. I mean, how would she get the chance? We've never met."

Timbers remembered a cosy evening in Ma's front room. The lights were off. Ma was in her armchair, smoking her pipe, and Timbers, sitting on the hearth rug and close to the older woman's feet, was eating buttered hot teacakes. Ma spoke about her friends who had worked on the streets before Timbers came to Goodladies Road. She told stories about the girls in the war. And she offered the wisdom that Timbers was too old (she was thirty-six, not forty) to stand on a street corner when younger, prettier girls were out to catch the same blokes. An old tart needs to find peculiar ways, Shippe had said, or peculiar gents. Timbers could no longer expect big breasts and a firm bottom to earn her bread without a little extra help.

How much of that lesson had reached Adcum Ops ears?

"I've heard that she was in the Hoboken Arms one night," Timbers explained. "The drink got the better of her tongue and off she went. One name after another. Old Elsie and Rosie Ditchen. Me and her young Baz. Daphne Butts who was murdered under the railway arches and Annie Ankers before the war."

But the senior policeman was burdened with his thoughts and Timbers wondered if he had heard anything of what she had said. Then, his face still staring through the windscreen, he said quietly, "I don't go in the Hoboken Arms. Whenever I'm in Goodladies, I sit in the car and wait for you."

"Maybe you're both right, you and Ma. Maybe, I should stop

working on the streets and become a full-time mistress for a special bloke. What do you think? Would you have me?"

"Timbers, I'm in trouble," he confessed. "I'm linked to a case that has gone badly wrong. People are out to get me – people close to my Chief, I mean – and I've no-one I can talk to. Except you, perhaps. That's why I've brought you up here."

'So,' thought the girl, 'the answer's no. So, you don't want me as your mistress.'

"Have you heard of the Tricorn?" he asked.

"Is it a name for the new supermarket?"

"More importantly, it's a new weapons system. There's talk that someone is going to steal it."

"Pinch a load of bombs and missiles?"

"More likely, the codes for working it; a set of books full of serial numbers in groups of five and seven. Information about an enemy plot was coming through Sergeant Bulpit. I was his controller. He gave me the information and I passed it to something called the Tricorn Security Committee." He paused, tapping the stalk of his cigar on the steering wheel. For a moment, Timbers thought that he was holding back tears. "Ned Machray has been a curse. I accommodated him in Shooter's Grove because I wanted someone to caretake the Civil Defence facility in the attic, but everyone says I've simply handed him an easy number. They scoff at his Police Dance Orchestra, make up stories about toy train sets in the old classrooms, and every time that his appalling attendance is mentioned, they look at me. Oh, our Chief Constable supports me. He supports Ned, as well you know, because of his war work. So, the Chief gave me this important job, the Tricorn Case, but people have been waiting for me to make a mistake. And now, Bulpit is dead. They'll say that I forced him to take too many risks. You see, we know that his wife is part of the plot to steal the secrets. That's why she murdered him. I should have seen it coming."

"But you don't know that she murdered him," argued Timberdick.

"As good as. She had the best motive and she's not been seen for three days."

"Perhaps the real murderer killed them both. Mr and Mrs Bulpit, dead in one go."

"God, don't tell me that. Lord, that would land me in more trouble. No, she'll turn up; we'll charge her and she'll be convicted. But sending Mrs Bulpit to prison won't save my skin, I'm afraid. The hounds are on the scent, dear Timberdick, and I'm their quarry."

He brought his fingers to his lips and gave a polite moan, not really a grunt. "Hmm. I need you to excuse me," he said, opening the car door. "Please, I'm sorry. It's not something I usually do, not at all. I'll make sure you won't see anything."

Timbers knew that this was the moment to talk about Mrs Bulpit's murder. This man would respond like a policeman – how could she expect otherwise? – but he would give her a hearing and he'd be fair. He wouldn't badger her and he'd allow her to give her account in her own time and her own voice. She saw his reflection in the passenger's vanity mirror as he rustled in the gorse bushes behind the car. In a few minutes, her chance would be gone; he'd come back to the car and the mood would move on. She needed to find the first few words, that's all, the rest of the story would follow. As she got out of the car, her panic rose. She saw the pictures in her head. The glass bottle, the stab wounds, the look on the woman's face, the lights in the hospital – each cluster of bulbs representing a dead body from her past. But she was determined to tell.

"Great Heavens! What are you doing?" He kept his back to her. "I'm spending a penny, Timbers. I didn't mean you to follow me."

"Please."

"No! Nothing like that. No, I must insist. Go back to the car."

And Timbers knew that the moment to tell the truth had gone for ever.

Now that the last of the busy, noisy cleaners had gone home, leaving all the doors bolted, the lights out and the alarms set, Peregrine 'the Popinjay' came out of the gentleman's toilet on the first floor and walked carefully through the sombre passageways, his troll-like ears pricked for any hint that he wasn't alone. He passed the glass cabinets of stones and bones on the landing and the narrow gallery of tapestry and needlework that linked two main exhibition halls and he found the little alcove, almost a room on its own, unbothered, unremarked and unmolested. A leather armchair waited in a corner with a low occasional table and old numbers of Studio arranged in a fan. A track of old stair carpet ran between the paintings and the chair. Peregrine had never seen anyone looking at the picture or sitting in the armchair so he supposed that the stretch of second-hand rug did its job very well. It hurried people past.

HMS Tricorn, a first rate from Nelson's day, was beating up the English Channel in a storm. The half light and treacherous shadows of the museum corridors seemed ideally appropriate for the painting. Leaning forward, Popinjay could barely make out the colour and bearing of the seasoned Captain on the quarterdeck. The figure was implied by just three or four strokes of the artist's finest brush. This matchstick man had to battle against the weight and power of the grey rolling seas – great chunks of oils from a pallet knife. It was an uneven fight but the seafarer's spirit saved it from being a forlorn hope. Popinjay savoured the rugged sturdiness of the sailing ship. He could feel the aching limbs of the sailors, drenched in salty seawater, cut and bruised from working with the ropes, canvas and oakwoods of Olde England.

PART TWO

TWO ENDS OF A TETHER

SEVEN

The Evidence of Peregrine Popinjay

Someone looking down on our city that night – perhaps the cats on the rooftops or the ravens in church spires, or the nightwatchman drinking tea in the hut on the top of the Co-Op's high building – would have had chance to observe some naughty characters sneaking about in the small hours.

Smee Ditchen, of course, and her live-in lover. They were pretending to be on their way home from the pictures but, really, they just liked kissing in the streets after dark. Smee's husband, Art, lived in the garden shed and when the lovers were out late, that night, he crept into the kitchen and stole from Smee's pantry, something he had promised never to do again.

My kitchen light went on at half past one. I had spent the day in bed, having set up the record player so I could play jazz records without leaving the blankets. I had to stretch to load the autochanger but, really, that was no problem. No wonder I was hungry in the middle of the night. I crept downstairs and treated myself to a fruit cake that had been maturing in its tin for three months. I found some nice damson jam to go with it.

At the same time, Timberdick was undressing in the dark while the Assistant Chief Constable (Admin-cum-Ops) was driving home. The ACC had the World Service on but Timbers, in two shakes of a cat's whiskers, had nothing on at all. She sniggered in the cold bedroom, then squirrelled inside Ma's sheets. Ma Shipley in the night-time smelt 'old fashioned pink', a mixture of too much talcum powder, Camay soap not properly washed off and Eau de Cologne that had been saved in a drawer for years.

The museum should have been the quietest place of all but Popinjay grew careless as the night wore on. He moved about, turned taps on and off and pulled the chain several times. He even sat on the back balcony when he wanted a break from watching HMS Tricorn. But the cats and the ravens weren't alarmed; there was something very normal about Popinjay trespassing at night.

The Co-Op's nightwatchman did notice a light in Smithers old garage and he thought it was strange because the place had been closed for five years, but he didn't know who was in there.

Stacey All-Night, smelling of old smoke and gin cocktails, poked the knife under the young Paul Tucker's nose and laughed at his nerves. He flinched but he had to trust that she was joking because he couldn't jerk backwards. The tennis ball, forced into his mouth, had already pushed his head as far back as it would go and his ankles and wrists were tied to an old office chair. The knots didn't bother him but he had been held here for forty minutes and he had worked out that the chair legs weren't even and he needed to twist his back to keep steady. His muscles were starting to scream. The tennis ball was caked with grease and oil from a vehicle pit. He wanted to be sick.

The girls had locked him in the back room of the old garage. The walls were cladded with hardboard panels, crudely painted yellow, and the only light in the place was yellow. It came from a fly spotted bulb a few inches above the boy's head. A glamour calendar, open at September '63, was pinned skew-whiff on the wall and an old wireless set sat on top of a battered filing cabinet. Something inside had blown, terminally, but anyone interested could have followed the flex behind the cabinet, through one hole in the skirtingboard and out of another and behind the desk until it reached the plug socket. Now and then, the wireless crackled and Tucker wondered if thunder and lightning were overhead. He hated thunder and lightning.

Stacey had one leg on the table top and the other stretched out to the floor. Her skirt was screwed up, she had one shoe off and her neck was red from struggling with the young man. She and Layna Martins had tied him up. Layna had gone for Slowly Barnes (she'll be good as this, she'd said), leaving Stacey in charge.

She laid the knife aside and tried to smile sweetly. "I'm not like the others," she began.

"Leave her alone, I said!" shouted Ma Shipley as she stormed through Smithers workshop. "Don't go bothering her, I said. Slowly's doing something important and you're all to leave her alone. And what do I hear? In the middle of the night? Cocky Miss Martins has gone round her house and asked her to come out!" She filled the office doorway.

"For Chrike's Sake, untie him! What is this? Ma Grissom's Gang? Get that stupid tennis ball out of his mouth; he looks like a pig dressed up for someone else's supper." While Stacey got busy with the lengths of old string, Ma clambered onto the desk and sat directly in front of the youth. When he was free, she put the sole of one foot on each of the chair's arms and sat with her grandmother knees apart; her jaundiced eyes – which matched the nicotine stains on her thumbs – challenged him to look up her old fashioned petticoat but he didn't dare. She hummed loudly and she lit her favourite old pipe, then leaned forward so that every puff blew smoke into his face.

"We call my daughter Baz but I wish we didn't. Why can't we call her Beryl, that's her name? She's in prison. Did they tell you that?"

The worried boy shook his head, his eyes fixed to her stare.

"Stacey says you know," Ma prompted.

"No. Honestly."

"Miss Martins says so too. They both say you talked about it."

"No. They didn't understand me. This is all a mix up, please."

"You see, somebody told Boots Leonard that my Beryl had told on him, got him arrested and charged and sent to gaol. And Boots? Well, he made sure that the other women in her prison heard the story. So, this morning, my Beryl – my daughter, you get me – was taken from prison to hospital because her face had been so badly cut."

77

His head was still wagging from side to side. "I don't know anything about any of that."

"You see, I need to know who told Boots, but Boots is dead, so I have to listen to everyone else. Who told Boots that my little girl was a grass?"

"I don't know."

"But you could find out."

At last, Master Tucker saw a way out. "Yes. Yes, I work on a newspaper and I can ask around the office. I can find out for you."

Ma Shipley fussed with her pipe.

"I won't let you down, Miss."

"You come back here, midnight, in four days time. Exactly when Friday turns into Saturday and we'll hear what you've got to say."

He nodded.

"That's when we'll decide," said Ma, finishing off.

He nodded but then didn't understand, so he frowned.

"Decide what to do with you," Ma explained. "You see this girl out here? Stacey, she's young and pretty. Well, apart from her face. I've always thought that it's pimply. What do you think?"

He didn't answer.

"But she's pretty enough for men to want to make love to her. Have you ever done that? Made love to a woman?"

He shook his head.

"Then Black Layna Martins would be too rich for you. Make sure you choose one like Stacey. You'll look after him, won't you Stace? Make sure he keeps on the straight and narrow? We don't want him going astray, you know what I mean? Now, Pauli, you go wary of the other one, called Slowly. She's older and heavier and has to find other ways to please men. Do you want to know?"

He went on shaking his head. But that gave Ma no cue to go further, so his shake turned into a nod and then became a wandering sort of movement that was neither a nod nor a shake.

"She whips men, whips them within an inch of their lives. I've heard that she cuts things off them. Really, people say that she does."

Ma Shipley looked closely at his tortured face, then threw her head back and roared with laughter.

The front garden of the city's museum was dripping wet. The early morning mist had lifted but left the leaves heavy with dew and a moist film across the bench that I had chosen. I noticed a rag, screwed up at the bottom of a drainpipe and I could have used it to wipe the seat, but I drew back from picking it up. I sat down and, as the damp soaked through my trousers, I shuffled a little and told myself to get used to it. Behind me, the corporation gates were locked but, next door, the forecourt of the bus depot was open to all and a forklift tractor was chained to the railings. I had clambered onto this stalwart and climbed over the fence. That was twenty minutes ago. Since then, I had finished a pipe, considered the beauty of wild fruit trees at the dawn of Spring and wondered why, no matter how blackened the bricks get, the red never stops trying to break through. I heard a twin prop aeroplane climbing as it began its journey north from a local aerodrome. How many people knew that this old Devon plane flew over six hundred miles to Abbotsynch every Monday morning? Stand-by Moreton had explained it to me when we were sitting on the seafront, two years ago. "The Navy has to fly it each week or they'd lose their slot in the air traffic schedule. They probably send a junior officer with a bunch of papers that he brings back on Wednesdays." Ever since, I had kept my eye out for it, if I was up early. This morning the sky was so clear that I could follow the metal bird's progress until it disappeared beyond the phoney horizon of the city's tall buildings. The road sweeper got to the bus depot at a quarter to six. He unshackled his cart from the fence and took up a whistle as he wheeled it along the road behind me. In an hour's time, he'd be fed up with whistling and the more attentive of pedestrians would make out a wheezing version of Londonderry Air under his breath, his dogged persistence making up for the infidelity of his pitch. The sweeper was hardly clear of the gates before the early morning crew arrived; the big doors of the garage rolled back and, calling and laughing to each other, they got the first bus going. I checked my Orient Express pocket watch. I might have to wait another two hours before any museum staff arrived. I recharged my pipe and settled against the back struts of the bench. I thought I saw a weasel slip out of the mortar, low down in the museum wall, and dart across the stony path to the rough shubbery. She was gone, and even if I had a mind to search for her, I knew that she wouldn't be seen again until the night-time.

Popinjay emerged not, like the weasel, from a crack in the mortar and not, like the roadsweeper, with the notes of Danny Boy at his lips but, like a magician, from the rockery that obscured the curator's ornamental pond. He settled himself beside me, making sure that his curious hat was safely in place before he asked, "How did you know?"

"Timberdick worked it out. She saw you walking down to the Early Bird Restaurant with your indoor hat and jacket on, like now, and you had some dead leaves from the corner bush on your shoulders. She can be quite a Sherlock Holmes when she sets her mind to it."

"Poppycock!" he blurted. It seemed the ideal exclamation to come from this fussy eccentric. "The spindly trollop saw my exit via the fire door, two weeks ago. What nonsense, and Timberdick didn't tell you anything; you've fallen out."

I explained with a smile, "Betty Barnes comes round to my place, most Monday mornings. She'd got the story from Timbers and passed it to me."[2]

"Ah, Betty Barnes." He inhaled, as if the name had an invigorating scent. "The one they call 'Slowly'. I've not really met her." A heavy lorry was passing the museum gates and he waited for the noise to die down before declaring, "I've done nothing wrong, Constable Machray. I've not taken anything."

"I know that you wouldn't do that, Perry. I think that you've been enjoying a last few chances to see your favourite painting before it's moved."

---

[2] This wasn't the only story of Timberdick's recent detective fantasies. Another story relied on her knack of remembering people by the words they used. So, the man behind the Post Office counter became the no-ifs-and-buts man. When Stacey All-Night lost thirty shillings from her purse, Timberdick said the thief was a Friday night bloke who finished each sentence with 'sort of thing'. But no-one else had heard of him and Stacey had never been robbed on Goodladies Road. It was all Timberdick's nonsense.

He nodded. "I feel good about it now. The Royal Navy Library will appreciate it far more than this museum's public. I've written, asking the officers to place it well. Well appointed, that's what it needs. I'm not worried, not now." He added with a twinkle, "I'm sure Peregrine the Popinjay will find a way in to see it."

"So, you're not angry about the transfer?"

"I never have been," he insisted. "That's just a story that Ma Shipley put about. No, it's quite right that a space is made for the street scene showing Widow McKinley's good work." His body leaned a couple of inches towards me. "Let me tell you something profound."

Profound?

An early morning wagtail landed on the path, less than a dozen paces away, pecked three times at the dirty tarmac, then darted away.

'Profound?' I repeated in my head. Mr Peregrine the Popinjay was such a superficial, fancy-headed chap that I doubted if anything deep and meaningful had ever passed between his ears.

"The Chairman of the Hanging Committee is the irritant. She has always complained about the picture of Widow McKinley. Yes, your Chief Constable's wife."

"She's only married to an Assistant Chief Constable," I corrected, adding "The Chief Constable's wife is an altogether different kettle of fish," but hoping that he would make nothing of it. "Your Madam Chairman is married to the Assistant Chief Constable, Adminstration-cum-Operations."

"The one they call Adcum Ops?"

"Yes. You should say Ops as if it's his surname and use Adcum for his first name. The canteen ladies thought it up and he's been at his desk for so many years that he has no chance of separating himself from the nickname."

"Ah, so that makes our Madam, Lady Adcum Ops."

"I suppose so," I said.

"And Betty Barnes? What makes her 'Slowly'?"

"The first fellow who begged her to beat him couldn't cope with her enthusiasm. 'More Slowly,' he kept shouting, but she thought he was calling her 'Slowly' and asking for 'More'. The story made her famous along the Goodladies Road in the 1950s."

He dipped his chin to show that he understood.

"So why are you here, Constable Machray? What," he hesitated as a scholar might do before quoting something classical, but all he said was, "brings you here?"

"You told Dave the Taxi Man about a commotion in the school hall two nights ago."

"Do you know what's happening in that place?" he asked. "Do the authorities know? Some people call it the Cockleshells Club. Ma Shipley sits upstairs with her jumble sale but, in the cellar, it's no more than a knocking shop for old men in search of strumpets. Scottish Carter behaves like a janitor but I think he has more to answer for. On Sunday night, I heard him and the Bloated Boy shouting their heads off. I don't think that they came to blows but it was a fierce argument, certainly. About one o'clock, I saw Ma Shipley turn up but she was only there for five minutes before she hurried off. She didn't want to get involved in the row, I supposed."

"You said that she ran the 'front' upstairs?"

"But she went home from those duties about half past twelve or, I should say, she went somewhere. I know not where for certain."

"And Timberdick?"

"I didn't see her. She was there early on, with your Betty girl, but I didn't see them come or go. I was sitting at my bedroom window, looking down on the street most of the time."

"And what was the argument about?"

Popinjay tugged at his ear for a couple of seconds. "I'd say a woman. Carter wanted to be rid of her. He said he was running away but the Bloated Boy wanted him to stay. 'You can't go until you've paid her the money,' I remember him shouting."

"When did they leave?"

"The Bloated Boy went first, two o'clock or thereabouts. I can't say for the other individual. I can't say."

"Was anyone else there? What about Boots Leonard?"

"I wouldn't know him, Mr Machray. I've heard talk of him, of course, but I've never seen him. I saw no-one else, except Ma Shipley again. She came back with cleaning buckets and mops on a barrow, about three or quarter past. This time, she stayed for half an hour or more."

He wanted to leave.

I said, "You can't have been at the window all the time, not if you spoke to Dave the Taxi Man."

"Well, no," he stumbled. "Well, yes. I came downstairs to see if any of my cats wanted to spend the night indoors. That's when I saw David parked at the kerb. That's when I spoke to him. But I could see the school hall all the time, couldn't I? And the lady doctor, she was there, sitting on the steps of the old school, taking her shoes off and rubbing her feet. That would have been ten minutes after Ma left."

"But Doctor Deborah was at the hospital. She tended Timbers."

"Yes, well, this was after."

Popinjay sensed my uneasiness that he wasn't telling me all that he knew. He enjoyed this one-upmanship for a few moments. "I suppose, if we were serious," he said, examining two fingernails as he clicked one over the other. "That is to say, a serious detective – one who wanted to do more than public service required – would begin with the will."

I laughed at that. "Boots Leonard was a tearaway. He'd have nothing to leave in a will."

"People say that he came into a great deal of money when he was eighteen," he reminded me. "Most of it, he wouldn't have been able to touch until the last couple of years so it could still be waiting in a bank, dry and dusty, looking for a suitor."

"However much it was didn't keep him out of gaol," I remarked.

Popinjay agreed and we both sat nodding to emphasise the point. He put the fingernails away and craned his neck, pretending to look for the wagtail on the museum's guttering. He sighed and mumbled incoherently before bracing his shoulders and proceeding with the smugness of a bridge player laying down his best trick. "I happen to know that there is a will. I was sitting at my upstairs window one night two weeks ago, watching, as Boots argued with that young copper of yours."

"I thought you hadn't set eyes on him?"

"I didn't. He was standing under the window. I couldn't see him but I could hear him. Mr Machray, are you trying to trip me up?"

"No. I want to be sure what you're telling me."

"Then concern yourself with the will, not with me. Now, as far as I know, the scallywag had no family so it would be interesting to find out who gets the money. Because whoever does surely has a motive for murder."

I thought it unlikley. "The will can't account for two deaths. I still think Boots was killed because he knew too much about the murder of Ronnie Bulpit."

"I see. You're the policeman, not me." But he had no doubt that I was wrong.

I got to my feet. "I'll look into it," I promised. "I know a librarian at Police Headquarters; he's expert at digging around without drawing attention to himself."

The city was awake now. Buses were drawing up at the museum stop and office workers were marching towards the commercial centre or one of our two railway stations. Three girls, already beyond their start time, dipped into a paper bag of sweets and they hurried, giggling, across the road to the clothing factory. PC Hobley, who had been told to spend the first part of his shift on the road between the Registry Office and the Harbour Ferry, came out of the Early Bird Restaurant, where he had sat for the past forty minutes, and headed off to the station and his breakfast break.

The soil and suds of the bed-bath stewed in three washing-up bowls on the carpet. Betty 'Slowly' Barnes, who had done all the work, stood at the bedside and dried up to her elbows with the last tea towel. Then, without thinking, she wiped it around her face; she checked herself, smelled the towel and pulled a face, twisted it into a thong and whacked it across the tender white meat of the Bloated Boy's bottom. He didn't make a sound but Slowly saw him try to lift his pelvis from the mattress and she guessed that he was wishing she'd do it again. His big bare body was face down on the bed, his head turned away from her, his legs apart and his ankles and wrists hanging limply over the edges of the mattress. His back was huge, sparsely haired and crevised like a rugged desert where dirt had lived for days (weeks, probably) because the boy's arms were too short for his body and he couldn't reach to wash. The great carcase from his legs to his neck pushed everything else into odd proportions. He had no shoulders to speak of. And, just below his knees, his legs were so thin that you'd think they'd snap beneath the weight that they carried. The great back seemed to have left no room for a properly shaped bottom. It had been pushed down and underneath so that his dimpled buttocks were like little suet puddings. The line between them curled like a comma and ended up going nowhere. Slowly looked at it and gave it second thwack with the tea towel. Very hard, this time, and the Bloated Boy grunted.

Slowly was a fat bottomed woman with muscled shoulders and feet made for stamping. Some people said that she moved like a poorly horse, others said that she walked as if she had clammy knickers (Timbers was one who said that). But old Ma Shipley said (and being Ma Shipley, she had said it to the woman's face, many times) that Slowly didn't walk at all but "waddled like an arse heavy duck".

She knocked into furniture as she picked things up and put things down, searching the carpet. "Everything will be all right now," she promised. "Ma and I will look after you."

She picked up the tin of baby talc, then hitched up her skirt so that she could climb onto the elephant's back. Her knees pressed into his bones as she powdered him.

EIGHT

The Hanging of Widow McKinley

Albert, the attendant, was the first to suggest that Timbers should join in the hanging. "Don't talk nonsense, you won't be out of place. You were close to the old lady before she died. You should be here when her picture is unveiled. Look, if you're nervous, why not come as one of our volunteers. I'm sure Mona would welcome some help in our little cafe."

Timbers took his comments home but did nothing with them. She hid behind the excuses of having nothing to wear and needing people to look after Li'l Timms.

"They won't expect you to dress up," said Slowly when, two days after the bodies had been found, the girls were sitting on the cemetery wall at one in the morning. "You'll get overalls from the cafe and who cares what's underneath? And the baby's no problem. Bring her round ours. We'd love to have her for the night." She read Timbers' dubious face. "Look, you know I'm hiding the Bloated Boy. It's supposed to be a secret but I reckon Ma's told you."

"I'll have to ask Ma," Timbers said as Slowly knew she would do. "Ma has the say-so about the Littl'un."

The museum's cafe was a kitchen with a hatch where staff usually queued in the corridor to collect sandwiches, lunches made with water from the kettle, and snacks toasted under a domestic grill. When the building opened its doors, after hours, four tables with chairs were placed in the passage and pedestrians were asked to avoid the cafe's customers by calling the cargo lift, normally kept for transporting artifacts. Timbers wanted to do the washing up, out of sight, but the other two ladies said she looked good on her feet so they asked her to ferry the dishes between the hatch and the tables. "Don't worry," they said. "People are usually very nice when they come to our evenings." They promised that they would all go upstairs, when the speeches were done, and watch the ceremony.

I was outside and across the street. I knew that the taxi would drop Popinjay at the bus depot so I decided to stand at the Early Bird Cafe and shout him when he arrived. Instead, Ma Shipley knocked into me from behind. She looked pale and washed up. She said she'd been sick in the toilet and wanted to talk to me. I said we'd have coffee together.

"Do you want an omelette?" she asked.

"Me want one?"

"Looking at cooked yolk settles my stomach. I can't explain it but it seems to help."

I said OK, I'd eat omelette. "Can I take anything in it?"

She called out, "Cook him a ham omelette. Not fluffy." She explained, "It has to be flat, like dough."

"Oh, good," I said but I didn't mean it.

We sat at a table, well to the back, and she told me to shut up. "Dr Deborah wants me to make a speech when they unveil the picture. Your Chief's wife was supposed to do it ..."

"The Assistant Chief's wife, you mean."

"I said shut up, Ned. Keep quiet." Her fingers were shaking on the table top, her voice was ready to falter. "God, I'm nervous. What am I going to say? The Adcum Ops Lady would be used to all this but she hasn't turned up and Dr Debs wants me. She says people know I was Maggie McKinley's best friend and she says that's just the job. What am I going to say?"

"Tell them the old bird had the cutest whores for hire in the back of her Curiosity Shop until a man was murdered on the stairs."[3]

---

[3] In 1982, my daughter researched the history of McKinley's old shop for a sixth form project. Her work focused on the architectural pedigree of the building but, nearly thirty years later, she remains convinced that Mrs McKinley knew little of what the girls did in the back of her shop, and that the building's place in history rests on far more than the murderous account in *Piggy Tucker's Poison*.

"Should I say that?"

When she took me seriously, I realised the state she was in. I steadied her hands. "Then say that she delivered hot potatoes and soup on a barrow to the poor in the blitz."

"The poor and the petrified," she nodded.

"Were you there that night in the picture?"

"There were many nights, Ned."

"But the night in the picture, with the children around the abandoned coach and the housewife serving supper from her handbarrow?"

"And the orange and reds in the sky, lighting up the line of the different shaped roofs. Yes, Ned, don't let anyone tell you it didn't happen or that's not Maggie McKinley in the picture because I know it was."

"It was the night they bombed the Guildhall?" I asked.

"They destroyed so much. I'll always remember the small, ordinary people who did their best with such little help. Just where that picture is, not twenty minutes after, I found a young woman – say, half my age as I was then . She'd been with others in Timothy Whites' cellar when the shops all around were hit and Timothy Whites fell to pieces. When she got out with her baby, a policeman – just standing on his own (that's what she kept saying, 'He was just standing on his own') – he told her to make her own way to the safety hall. She'd walked for three miles when I found her. With her baby in her arms and the bombs still falling and everywhere burning. Buildings all around her were on fire. Some walls fell down. Some craters in the road were so big that you could fit trucks in them. She thought that her baby was dead but she kept walking. Three miles. Well, when we got her to the reception centre and got the baby washed, she was fine. But when I kept asking about the other people in the cellar, the young woman wouldn't answer. 'There was nobody else when I got out,' she kept saying, 'so something must have gone on with them.' 'I never saw,' was all she'd say. God knows what the poor woman had seen."

I knew that her mind was back in those days. Tears were in her eyes but she saw the images clearly and she spoke so certainly, never wanting to correct a word, that the story seemed to tell itself.

"Just tell them about the war, Ma. They'll want to listen."

The owner brought omelettes on two plates, slices of buttered bread and a pot to refill our coffee cups. He took the cigarette from his mouth so that it wouldn't shake ash onto the plates when he spoke. "I got some nice cake," he said.

"I don't want to eat omelettes," Ma explained. "I want to watch him eating. That's what settles my stomach."

He looked at me, I nodded, and he slid the second omelette onto my plate. "You want both breads too?"

"Go on, then. With some ketchup."

"Yeah? You think I'm here to fetch and carry for you? You take a bottle from the other tables." He put the fag back in his mouth and went off to the kitchen.

"You don't think I should mention Maggie McKinley's husband then?"

I said with my mouth full, "I think you should tell them what happened in the Cockleshells Club on Sunday night."

That scared her. "Is that why you got me in here?" she barked. "So that you can ask questions? We all know you want to cause trouble for Timbers."

"Hey, you asked me here. You wanted to watch me eat omelettes, remember?"

"It's over, Machray. She doesn't want you anymore. Don't think you can blackmail her into changing her mind. It won't work."

I put a clump of omelette on half a slice of bread and folded it into a sandwich. I looked at some egg poking through an opening, I wondered for a couple of seconds, then wiped it around the neck of the sauce bottle. "All right," I said. "Try telling me about the hanging committee."

"You know about that." She folded her arms and sat back in her chair. "Your Lady Adcum's the leader and Dr Debs is on it and some others. They decide which pictures go on the wall and which ones stay in the storeroom."

"You told them that Widow Mac should be on show?"

"No. It was Dr Debs, not me. You know all this, Ned Machray,

89

why are you making me go through it? Look, Dr Debs was in the courthouse when the judge sent my little girl down. She saw I was upset and sat with me for an hour or more. I got to talking about Goodladies Road in the old days and I told her about the painting I'd found in Maggie McKinley's Curiosity Shop. She was the one who said it should be hung. Your Adcum lady has been against it but the doctor won through."

She watched me pick the gooey sauce and dried yolk from the corners of my mouth. "It was never going to be a happy mix, that one," she said.

"Very tasty. Thanks, Ma. Thanks a lot."

"I mean Dr Debs and Adcum's Lady Muck. The doctor's a Ban the Bomb girl, you see. She does the Alderman's March."

"Aldermaston."

"Whatever you call him. And she writes Vietnam stuff."

"Good Lord," I said. "Lady Adcum Ops wouldn't approve of either. Protest and petitions curry no favour in her circle."

"Ned, I've seen the look on her face. She has the look of a lady who'd like to teach a good learning to the doctor, if you get my meaning. She'd like to put a wrong girl right in an unfriendly sort of way."

I did some thinking aloud. "Dr Deborah was there when Timbers was taken to the Royal Infirmary."

"Yes, Dave the Taxi Man will have told you that. She was off duty and they called her in when Timbers played up."

"Yes," I played back to her. "Dave the Taxi Man. He saw Popinjay outside the Cockleshells Club and Timbers in the street. And Dr Debs and Boots Leonard in the hospital; even Mattie Hughes bounced off his bonnet. A man could say that the Taxi Man has seen most of it." I asked, "Who killed the Bloated Boy?"

"How the hell should I know!" Then her mouth dropped and a hand went to her forehead. "Oh God, is he dead too?"[4]

"He's not been seen since Sunday. That's the night Ron Bulpit

---

[4] I have to say, her acting was good.

was killed. Dave saw him too. He says Slowly was waiting for him in the scrap-merchant's cabin."

"Oh God. You mean PC Bulpit, Boots Leonard and the Bloated Boy – all dead?"

"And Amy Bulpit's not been seen either."

"You think she's dead?"

I shook my head. "No. What reason would anyone have for murdering Amy Bulpit? No, if anything, she's a suspect."

I had finished the supper. I put my head back and took in the last of the coffee. "Have we got time for another cup?" I looked around for the chocolate cake but saw no sign of it.

"You will write down what I've got to say, won't you?"

I grabbed a flimsy serviette and started to scribble some notes. "Just talk about the war, Ma. They'll love it."

"I thought that I might get some pocket money for doing it," Ma said. "But the doctor says Lady Muck can't pay me. It's against the rules."

I pulled out my wallet and took two pound notes from the sleeve. "Here, buy something for Li'l Timms."

"You're nice, Ned. Nothing like what the girls say about you," she said as she secured the money inside the top of her dress.

The early evening traffic was stopping and starting. Three trolley buses queued to park in the depot when there was only room for two. The Transport Manager was in the middle, waving his arms and shouting, and a bread van, having delivered six crates to the staff canteen, was trying to get out. A mechanic in blue overalls and steel-capped boots rushed into the Early Bird, yelling, "That's it! One more stupid order and I'll murder the dope!" Without waiting for a response, he stomped out.

Ma Shipley was too worried about her address to care about traffic jams.

Twelve good citizens witnessed the hanging of Widow McKinley. The alcove between two corners in a lobby at the top of a staircase allowed room for no more. I wasn't invited but they say that the ceremony went well and Popinjay was pleased to announce that

91

HMS Tricorn would now be more properly displayed in the Royal Naval Establishment.

When the witnesses joined us in the main gallery, Ma Shipley had already spent thirty minutes chatting about the old days, so she was well warmed up. She stood, gripping the lectern and not taking her eyes off the friendly faces in the front row. I don't think she used my notes at all.

Neither Ma nor Dr Deborah mentioned the absent wife of the Assistant Chief Constable but there was plenty of talk about her afterwards. She had objected to Widow McKinley's elevation to a local figure. She wasn't a worthy; she was a cheap scoundrel and the worst gossip on Goodladies Road. When Popinjay heard these grumbles he muttered that he couldn't understand the fuss because, as far as he was concerned, Widow McKinley wasn't even in the damned silly picture. "You've got better old masters in the attic of Shooter's Grove," he said. "Bring them down and let others enjoy them."

Popinjay was in an awkward mood that evening. He pinched the elbow of my sleeve while people were still clapping Ma and wouldn't let go until he'd taken me down to the make-do cafe. "We'll run the girl ragged," he said, meaning Timbers. "We'll change our order and complain about the tea, then we'll argue over the bill."

"We'll do nothing like that," I said. "This evening means a lot to people from Goodladies Road, so don't spoil it." I told him to look around. "Many of them have lived within sight of the Hoboken Arms all their lives. They don't get much to celebrate."

He laughed. "God, Machray. Just look at their lives; they should be ashamed to show up at a place like this. What's more, upstairs, it was a damned disgrace. That Martha Shipley used to be a brothel-keeper, ten times worse than old pussy McKinley, and I'm not sure she's much better now. She shouldn't be speaking at a public function. It's a damned disgrace, worse than a disgrace. Look, I don't mind policemen romping with these girls on nights, or shady ladies calling on you on Monday mornings ..."

"Hey! Steady on. Watch what you're saying."

"But I draw the line at madams speaking for the community in public places of learning."

When I reminded him that Ma Shipley had been Widow McKinley's best friend, he said sulkily, "It's not much of a picture, anyway. I can't see what all the fuss is about."

Timberdick was avoiding our table. She made sure that everyone else had been served, then collected their dead cups and saucers and replenished their sugar bowls before addressing us. She scribbled our order without a word and turned her back with a haughty trip.

"She's cross with me," I explained. "Even after all these weeks."

"Still, you must love it. Having her in a position where she's got to do things for you."

"What do you mean?"

"She's got to wait on you, Ned. Enjoy it."

"No, no. There was a bit of a mix up and she blames me. She was arrested for robbing in the street, although she was indoors when it happened. I got to hear about it three days later and I sort of assumed that it had been all sorted. Bugger it Pop, the Assistant Chief, a WPC and a probationer had been with me, looking out of the Hoboken's window and we all saw it happen. It was Baz Shipley who 'dunnit'. Not Timbers. But by the time I got to the magistrates, she had already been remanded for seven days."

"In prison? She went to prison for seven days?"

"She did. For seven days, until the truth came out."

"So little Baz Shipley went to prison because you told on her?"

"Yes. I mean, of course. I'm a policeman."

"Ma Shipley must be angry about that."

"Pretty cross, I suppose. But I wish Timbers wasn't. She thinks that I deliberately kept quiet to get my own back."

"Revenge, because she turned you down?"

"Yes, but she didn't turn me down because I didn't propose in the first place. Timberdick suggested that we should get married and I said yes because I knew she would change her mind. And that's what happened."

"Quite right too. Betty Slowly Barnes is much more your size."

"What do you mean? Nothing's going on with Betty."

He made a face. "But to leave Timbers in prison for seven days, that's ..."

"Look, I didn't know until the Wednesday. We were at a Cliff Richards weekend."

Another face.

"Me and Slowly were," I said with my chin down. "Pop, I want you to pass a message to her."

"Don't call me Pop," he complained. "It makes me feel old and friendly, like a sad chap in an allotment shed. Popinjay's fine, or Peregrine. I mean that is my name, after all, Peregrine. Perry, too. I quite like Perry."

"Tell Timbers that I want to meet her."

"Tell Timbers? She won't take anything from me. Tell her yourself."

"I can't, can I? She won't even look at me properly. Look, tell her to meet me at the top of Cardrew Street at two this morning."

"Tell her yourself," he repeated.

"No. I'll wander off, then you can catch her eye and say I'd left a message for her. She's to meet me at two o'clock at the top of Cardrew Street. Tell her it's important and tell her to come dressed for burglary."

I slipped away. I thought I could avoid the clutch of people admiring the painting by heading for the back of the ground floor. It was quiet and empty in that part of the building.

I opened a door and saw a narrow passage sloping down to the fire doors, some thirty yards away. It seemed like a good way out for someone who didn't want to be seen. The light switch didn't work but there was enough from the top corridor, so I stepped into the greyness. The air was heavy with carpet dust and the smell of old cobwebs. Half way down, the light faded and I drew a hand along the side wall to guide me. Twice I stopped; I thought I could hear something close – but I decided that it was a leaking pipe behind the ceiling and nothing for me to worry about. Then someone stood at the top entrance, all but blocking out my light.

"It's only me, Ned. Only, Ma. I wanted to get you alone."

She started to walk towards me and I had the stupid notion that, somehow, I was in danger. I didn't shout out 'Stop' or 'Keep your distance' but that's how I felt. "The party's still going on back there. I saw you wanting to slip away. Ned, you're wrong. I don't blame you for my Beryl getting caught. She did it in daylight in the middle of the street so she was bound to go to prison. I was surprised none of the other policemen spoke up before you did. And, anyway, we couldn't let Timbers get done for something Baz did. She should have owned up from the start."

"I can't get out of the doors," I called. "They're padlocked."

"That's what it says at the top. 'Do not use in case of fire.' 'No way out.' 'These doors are locked.' The trouble has always been that you should have spoken up sooner."

"I was away. You know that."

"And Timbers knows it too," said Ma. "You let her stay in prison while you and Slowly Barnes jollicked by the seaside."

"Ma, it wasn't like that."

I started to climb the slope towards her.

"Ma, I want to get a message to Timbers. Will you tell her?"

"Ned, I was wrong about you. I should push you and Timbers together, not drive you apart. She needs a fat slob in her life. Someone who is happy with meaningless things, whose days are full of little matters or no matter at all. She needs someone who is reliable, not bothered by any morals, but reliable because he has nowhere else to go, nothing else to do."

"I want her to help me with a job. Will you tell her a message?"

Still, she took no notice of me. Her little speech needed all of her attention, that was the trouble. "Timbers needs to have a nobody to fall back on, Ned, and that's you. It can't be me. I've got a mind of my own. I stand up for myself. Don't you see, you're perfect because you're too much of a slob to get out of the armchair. You're just the man Timbers needs."

I thought: Ned Machray, you're right. You are in danger.

When I left the museum, two police cars were parked across the bus depot entrance and a casualty was being lifted into an ambulance. The mechanic in blue overalls was sitting on the kerb and a copper from Central was standing over him. A Sergeant, notebook at the ready, walked up to me and said, "He went to the Early Bird Restaurant for help but everyone ignored him?"

"No, Serge. It was nothing as definite as that."

"Hmm," he said, tapping the biro against his teeth. "He says he told you that he was going to murder Mr Torrence and you did nothing about it."

"Well, not really. No, it wasn't like that."

"Do you want a word with him before he makes a statement?"

"No. I'll leave well alone."

"It is fortunate that the casualty hasn't died."

"Indeed, very fortunate."

"I mean, in the circumstances. I mean."

A dog handler shouted from the far side of the forecourt. "Your Governor wants to see you, Mach. He said on top of the Westminster." He made a show of checking his watch. "Round about now."

"Nonsense," burbled the Sergeant. "He means in the Westminster, not on it. You can't meet a man on top of a car." He closed his notebook. "You better get going. The HQ Westminster's parked at Central."

NINE

Trouble with Noises Off

I went nowhere near Central Police Station but headed through Cork Park. It's nothing like a park. It's a draught board of high rise flats separated by paving slabs, concrete benches and buzzing nests of communal waste bins. The open areas were quiet that night but I could hear people on the staircases and the landings or gathering in the smelly foyers at the bottom of the lift-shafts. I was on course for the London Road exit when someone, high up, shouted: "You're a dirty bastard Machray!" Twenty years policework had taught me not to turn around and look for catcallers but this one got to me. She sounded as if she meant it.

"What have you been doing to her," teased Alf Gillikin as he and his dog raced ahead of me. Fifty yards on, he glanced back and laughed.

I reached the Westminster Bank as the Guildhall clock was striking twelve. I checked that no-one was watching, then I slipped around the back where I could climb to the roof.

"Why are we meeting up here?" I asked, short of breath. The Westminster Bank on London Road had a flat roof with just a trim little balustrade to stop you falling off. Over the years, I had gathered some furnishings – a wooden beer crate for sitting on, a hessian sack for keeping newspapers dry – but it still didn't look like a camp. I was sure that no-one would suspect.

"I like it," said the Assistant Chief Constable. He kept his hands in his raincoat pockets and walked around in a circle. "Yes, the neighbourhood is laid out below so you can keep watch on your people and their properties without enforcing a presence. A bit like a kindly shepherd, I suppose."

"Who told you about it?" I asked

"Oh, you and the Westminster Bank are well known. I'm sure you've some beer bottles somewhere but I can't find them."

"Guttering at the back of the first floor keeps them cool. I hoist them up with bits of string."

He nodded and said, 'Very well,' like people in charge do. Adcum Ops looked spent and weary. His limbs seemed limp, his shoulders and knees were wobbly, his wrists twitched with nerves. But there was an old soldier inside him, always summoning one last effort. His face was ghastly – lined and grey, with weepy eyes in sockets that were red-sore. His clothes were fresh but they were half a size too big and he didn't have enough on under his coat. I found other tell-tale signs of the man's decline: although his shoes were brightly bulled, he hadn't been able to knot his laces precisely in the middle and precisely even as he used to do. Little signs like that. Up here, in the deceptive air of the early hours, with the sounds of the city seeming far off, he appeared even more isolated. Detached, almost. He was a man losing his grip.

"Have you ever thought?" He stepped to the edge of the roof and looked over. "Everything happens at ground level. They say that wars are fought in the air nowadays, but they're wrong. What planes do, happens on the ground. We can fly jets at the speed of sound and shoot rockets into space but everything still happens at ground level. You know, I think you're the greatest detective I've ever known."

I offered a little laugh as I reached for his coat sleeve. "Oh, I don't think so, Sir," I said. "I don't think you think that at all." I led him away from the edge and stood him over the beer crate until he relented and sat down.

"I'm not broken, Ned. I'm just tired."

"Perhaps we could go somewhere else to talk?" I suggested.

"I've always liked Shooter's Grove, you know."

"Yes, we could go there."

"I could sit in the garden, one afternoon, do you think that? PC

Machray, maybe I could help you straighten things. A little tidying up of the long grass. Pruning? What do you think? What would people say? We have to be so careful, these days, about what people make of things." He drew breath, said that he liked the cold and the night-time, then warned me, "The Estate Officer's coming to look at Shooter's Grove. The Chief has said that we need to assess all our properties with a view to best use."

"I guess the money's needed for the new Headquarters," I said, wanting to be helpful.

"Of course, I'll put up a good argument and Rowena's on your side. Always useful, having the Chief Constable's daughter on your side. But the thing is, they want to put Pandas in."

"Pandas, Sir?"

"Cars, Machray. Not bears."

"I know, Sir, but Pandas in Shooter's Grove? Surely not?"

He looked me straight in the eye. "Have you ever slept with them?"

"Pandas, Sir? You mean the bears?"

"Either one, I mean. Not both of them."

"It's nothing I've thought of," I said bewildered.

"Only we know that you're friends with Rowena and there's a story about you and her mother in the fifties."

"Good Lord, Sir. That's dangerous nonsense. Heavens."

"Good. I wouldn't want you to tell me, even if you did."

"Rowena has always liked me. She got me into Shooter's Grove and she convinced her father to give me the Police Dance Orchestra, but we've never been close."

"Good show," he said, picking at his fingertips.

"I mean, yes. I worked for the Chief's wife in '53 but there was never anything improper."

"Good, jolly good. I would rather you didn't tell me, even if ..."

"We didn't make love."

"Please, that's just what I want to hear. If you did, don't tell me."

"But we didn't."

"Good. Good, that's just the stuff."

I said 'but we didn't' one last time, then I gave up. Below us, the bored nightwatchman had been playing with the lift buttons. We heard the cables wind and rest and the gears gave a great clunk that shook the top of the building. "How are things, Sir?" I asked.

"The hounds are after me," he said. "I'm in a mess over Bulpit's death. The Chief has brought in a Superintendent from another Force to investigate and I like him, I do. He says it's unfair that I should take any blame. He says that the whole of CID's a mess. Have you heard, they've promoted that fool Moreton. I mean, how did that happen?" He added quietly, "Dog pooh. That's what he's famous for. Greater Attention to Dog Fouling. That was his idea. And have you heard his latest notion?"

I said that I hadn't.

"No smoking in shops. He's heard these scare stories about tobacco and he's proposing that we should ban cigarette smoking in shops. He says people will get used to going without and stop buying cigarettes completely. Well, I teased him. I said, why stop at shops? Why not ban smoking in pubs? 'Now you're making fun of me,' he said. And this man, this dreamer, is looking for Bulpit's murderer."

"Sir, I want you to go home." Carefully, I put a hand to the elbow of his coat sleeve and he let me guide him to the fire escape. "Times will always look better when a man has his family around him, you know. "

"Yes. Yes, I'm very lucky like that. I'd never do anything to hurt them."

"Then take care of youself."

At the top of the ladder, he paused, turned to face me and said, "Timberdick worries me most." He let the words lie a little, then asked, "You know that new Constable on Goodladies Road?"

"He's a good lad," I said.

"The night before Ron Bulpit was found, he saw a prostitute arguing with him at the junction of Cardrew Street. He thought it was about money, but he wasn't sure. At first, he couldn't identify the woman but 'Sergeant Moreton' – our Sergeant of the Dog Pooh – sat him in front of a table of photographs and he picked out Stacey All-Night. He was wrong. I know it was Timberdick Woodcock."

We climbed down in silence. He started to speak as soon as his feet were on the pavement and I had to catch up to listen.

"I want to share something with you, Ned. Maybe I shouldn't, but if anything happens to my position, I want to leave someone in the Force who knows the truth. The facts are these. I have been out of the county for a couple of days, checking on a road accident report in Bedfordshire. Odd behaviour for an Assistant Chief Constable, you're thinking? The casualty was Scots Carter. An old lady of eighty-six reversed over his body in a car park on the M1. I wanted to check that the eighty-six year old wasn't thirty and called Amy Bulpit."

"Why should Ron Bulpit's wife kill Scots Carter?"

"It goes back to 1959, well '57 really. A photograph appeared in a railway magazine showing spectators on the viewing embankment of Cryer's Hatch. Stand-by Moreton and Amy Bulpit were in the back row."

"That was a co-incidence," I said.

"Not really. They were in each other's arms. They didn't expect anyone to photograph them or their picture to appear in a magazine. They kept quiet and they thought they'd got away with it. But, two years later, the blackmail started. It seems that Stand-by paid up for the best part of a year before he went to the Chief. There was no investigation. Stand-by insisted on that, for Amy's sake. But we know the identity of the blackmailer."

"Scots Carter," I said.

"But Carter's death has nothing to do with Mrs Bulpit. I want you to know that, Ned. I don't want you to do anything, but I want you to know it."

He was across the street when he called back to me. "I have my family. Sometimes I think that's enough. Our eldest is doing well in the army and Marie is going up to university next year. It can be very satisfying, watching your grown-up family and realising that it's a job well done."

I shouted goodnight.

That was the last time I saw him. If I had known I would have turned to wave cheerio. Probably, I'd have watched him walk away, wanting to remember his steady stride with shoulders braced and head held high. But those days were out of reach.

It took me ten minutes to march to the top of Cardrew Street but I was still early. I rested against the wall of the corner house when one of the new girls appeared from the side street. She was carrying her sandals, her knees were red and her top was soaked. I was about to ask what had happened to her, when she shouted: "Get away from me! Filthy animal! You've got some arse, showing your face after what you said." And she ran to the other side of the road.

I couldn't make it out. First, a catcall from the Cork Park flats. Now the girls were disgusted.

I gave Timbers until twenty past. I thought she might be spying on me, testing how long I'd wait for her, but when Dave's taxi went past and his face had a look that said he'd remember me being there, I gave up on that thought too. Timberdick had stood me up. I collected my car from the back of the television repair shop and motored across the city to the military slopes where Dr Deborah lived. She had a square semi-detached in the middle of army married quarters so heaven knows how she got the lease. I had worked out that if I parked by the timber fence of the old tip, I wouldn't raise suspicion and could still reach it if I needed a quick getaway.

I knew that she was working until eight o'clock that morning but could be home any time after three if the doctors were cheating on their shifts. I wanted to find any evidence of her Aldermaston walks.

I was ready to poke the Somerset's distributor feeler gauge between the lock and the doorframe when the door opened and Dr Debs said: "Why Edward! What are you doing here?"

She wore a sloppy joe jumper and tights without a crinkle, a pushy bra but no skirt or slippers and she shouldn't have been here. I had prepared an excuse to offer nosy neighbours or sleepy dogwalkers, but I didn't have an answer ready for Deborah. I tried, "You're up late, Doctor. Is something wrong?"

"I'm on the sittingroom carpet, going through picture albums. I was hoping to find a photo of me and Constable Bulpit. We did the Aldermaston March together. So, why are you here, Edward?"

I said without thinking, "I couldn't sleep. I've been for a drive and a bit of a walk and I've ended up here. I saw your light on."

"Edward, I haven't got a light on. There's no need with the curtains open, the streetlamp's enough."

I stood there. I had no other explanation so she had to swallow my story or tell me to clear off.

"You'd better come in," she said.

The photograph album was open on the front room floor. She had pulled a cushion from an armchair so that she could be comfortable on the carpet and was using a folded magazine as a mat for her cup of coffee. Her slippers were discarded, upside down and a few feet apart.

I've always thought that there is something intimate about seeing a woman in her stockinged feet. It's not a thing that ladies do with strangers – take off their shoes. I tried not to look but the toes were perfectly matched, like spoons in a box, and the big ones had carefully shaped nails, a little longer than was tidy, with pearly varnish. That's what I saw through the nutty coloured nylons.

She sat down on the hearthrug, tucking the feet beneath her bottom, out of sight. "I suppose I ought to offer you something. Sherry's all I keep in. There's coffee and tea but it's such a palaver. You can make some yourself if you prefer."

By the time I had filled two glasses, she'd put the feet back on show. She was sitting with her knees up and her arms wrapped around her shins. The little piggies were flexing and wiggling and itching to play. She knew that I was bothered by them so she left them where they were, put her head to one side and smiled.

"We all thought that Ronnie was part of Special Branch."

"Why else would he march for Ban the Bomb?" I asked.

"But he never asked us questions. I suppose he was observing what went on and we did tease him. I made up stories that I'd been recruited by strange lefties at university."

"He would have been used to that," I said.

I was still standing up and she was still sitting down. That way, she could let her feet fidget and I was sure not to miss them. Sometimes, the underneaths (they weren't polite enough to be called

103

soles) showed themselves with plucky impertinence. Like naughty puppies yearning to be tickled.

"He did help me once," she said. "I'd lost a necklace that Daddy had given me for my twenty-first. Ronnie got it back for me. The Shipley woman had stolen it. She had to make all sorts of promises before he let her off."

"All sorts?"

"Look, I don't know the dirty details. Here he is." She held out the picture album. "See, that's me and my intended-for-the-day and Ronnie's just a bit, well, kind of between us."

"Did Ma Shipley talk to you about the necklace?"

"To be frank, Edward, I didn't consider the woman again until we met on the day of her daughter's trial. She didn't mention it then. Well, it happened so long ago, didn't it? But I got the impression that she was fed up with PC Bulpit." Then she said, "Can't you blame that horrible little man, Popinjay? Can't you make up a story that he murdered poor Amy?"

That made me look her straight in the face. "He didn't know her," I said simply, but that wasn't on my mind.

She put a hand in the air, wanting me to pull her from the floor but I didn't.

"Would you like me to stand on my dining table?"

"What on earth ..."

"Edward, it's a well known fact, 'a truth universally acknowledged', that gentlemen with a foot fetish — "

"I haven't got a foot fetish!"

"Gentlemen with a foot fetish like to see the objects of their desire on polished surfaces, like smoked glass, or mirrors on the floor, or the polished top of a dining table." She wagged her fingers. "Now, pull me up."

"This is ridiculous."

"You like looking at my feet, don't you?"

"Doctor ..."

"You know you can call me Debbie, Edward." She managed to stand up without my help. She told me I was a spoilsport with no sense of humour. "You do like looking at my feet."

"They're pretty enough," I replied. "But I don't want them in my head, day and night."

"And I like showing them to you. I think we'd both like it if I got on the table top."

"I shouldn't have come here," I said, returning the empty glasses to the sideboard. "You've told me all I need to know. You've said more than enough."

She was already standing on the dining chair and testing one foot on the table. "If you don't steady me, I shall fall," she demanded, holding her arms wide like a tight-rope walker.

I couldn't help thinking: this performance is the antic of a medical student. Bed-racing, bar-diving and now table-standing. I held her hand while she stepped to the middle. The table creaked and swayed a little but it carried her weight. I have to say, she was a sexy thing, standing like a centre-piece with her sweater and stockings, and her figure showing in all the places it should.

"There," she said. "What do you think?"

Her notion appeared to have some truth in it. Now that they were presented on a polished surface, her feet took on the stature of works of art.

"What shall we do, Edward?"

I couldn't help it. The pictures forced themselves into my head. I wanted to leave her there while I hurried to her kitchen. I would keep her talking while I prepared a plate of beans on toast. I'd come back. I'd sit at the table and eat it all up while her feet were displayed, just inches in front of my busy face. But I didn't do it.

Instead, I made my way to the front door.

"You pig. You're deserting me. Edward!"

I was on my way out when I turned to her and asked, "Who said Amy Bulpit was dead, Doctor?"

"Well. Well, nobody did. Nobody actually said it." She put both hands to her head. "Oh God, I'm such a dizzy."

TEN

The Leonard Legacy

Friday morning. Four days since I had found Boots Leonard's body. It was half past five and I hadn't been to bed. With a mug of tea and two biscuits, I dawdled to the bottom of the garden at Shooter's Grove and drew some fresh cold air into my lungs. Plenty needed doing to the shrubs and vegetables but I had to be careful. My sick note depended on a bad back and pulling pains in my legs; I didn't want to be caught out. A cooked breakfast in Jack's All Night Cafe seemed a good idea, so I left the house and walked through the quiet streets. Then I heard St Mary's chime the three-quarter hour and I remembered that Herbert Jayne always started work before six. I phoned him from the box on the corner of Cardrew Street.

"You were right, our Ned. Young Bootsie left a small fortune but it seems that he caught a bout of righteousness while he was doing time. Apart from two special bequests, he left his whole estate to St Mary's Church."

"To the church? Boots Leonard left his money to a church? I don't believe that."

"The story goes that they looked after him when he was down on his uppers. The old curate let him sleep in the vestry at night and gave him decent meals."

"When was this?"

"1960 and the start of '61."

"Thanks," I said, taking in the history.

"Do you remember I said there was a story about Amy Bulpit in '59?" prompted Herbie.

"I know all about that."

"You know Scots Carter's dead?"

"Adcum Ops briefed me on the Westminster roof. Look Herbie, thanks for your help."

"I'm not through with you yet, Ned. I said he left two special bequests. He wanted a caravan to go to the cats home on Anderton Street and then there's this boat, tied up at Foreshore Creek."

"Boat?"

"I'm holding a photograph of it. A motor cabin cruiser."

"Boots Leonard had a boat?"

"A modest job but it floats and it's got deisel in it, his solicitor says."

"You've spoken to his solicitor? Herbert, was that wise? We want to be careful about all this, remember."

"His solicitor was in touch with the Personnel Office yesterday."

"Why would he do that? Herbie, this isn't making sense. There's a lot more to it than I thought. Who'd he leave the boat to, Herb?"

"One of our own. One Ned Machray of this parish."

All was quiet in Ma's bed. Outside, cars were passing, milk bottles knocked into one another and the first of the children were on their paper rounds. The wild rose, which had taken up occupation, fracturing the brickwork of the coalhouse and refusing to die, brushed its stalks and thorns against the back door. Something similar, though Timbers didn't know what, was tapping on the window of Li'l Timms' nursery. But none of these nuisances mattered if Timberdick stayed, covered by blankets, in the cocoon of Ma's pink bed.

Heavenly. The talcum powder and the worn linen. The wishy-washy scent and the familiar warmth of the older woman's body. Timberdick was properly awake but she kept her eyes closed. If she opened them, she would not be able to pretend when the time came for Ma to tickle her into life.

"Don't fidget," Ma mumbled.

Timbers said nothing at first, wanting to insist that she was asleep, then she answered quietly, "I'm not."

"I can feel you wanting to, so I'm telling you not to."

Again, a moment's silence.

"It's morning, Ma."

"If you fidget, I shall pinch you hard."

"Just where my bottom finishes and my legs start," said Timbers, full of obedience.

"Just there, so don't."

"I'm not. I'm keeping absolutely still. I want to keep still. I don't want to fidget." But the spell had been broken and in the end she did.

Ma sat up and poked her fingers through her dry hair. "You need to make it up with Ned," she said, scratching.

"He's sulking."

"And you're being stubborn."

"Any case, not while he's spending too much time with Slowly."

"That's never bothered you before."

"It's didn't bother me because I was Number One. Now, it bothers me."

"You'll do as I say, Timberdick. That's always been in the rules."

Timberdick asked, "Are you thinking of throwing us out? Look, I know what people say, that I'm not good enough with the baby, that I dumped her onto you."

"Well, we know different, don't we? We know that you're helping me keep busy while my Baz is in prison. I adore Li'l Timms. In these last few days I can see when she recognises my voice. Her little shoulders go soft when she hears me, and she's beginning to tell me things in the different ways she cries. I never noticed those things with my Baz. Besides, bugger what other people say. Loads of grandmas look after the tiny mites round Goodladies. It's normal, Timbers."

"I'll tell them next time."

"Don't answer them."

"You're the nanny. I want us to stay here and I want you to take Timmy to the park in a big black pram so you can sit on the benches and talk to all the other nannies."

108

"And I'm telling you to make it up with Ned."

They sat on two corners of the mattress, halfway to getting up. Ma said, "We're broke, Timbs. I'd forgotten how much a baby costs. Don't worry, we'll get through it. I clawed two pounds from Ned last night and if you can find a bit more from somewhere?"

"I borrowed twenty-five bob from Slowly, although I should pay it back really. Maybe I can do a bit this afternoon." She sighed, "Used to be, I could always earn as much as we wanted but I've lost my way, I suppose. I'm not as good at it as I was. But I will, Ma. I'll snitch some blokes this afters."

Later, when Ma was picking Li'l Timms up from her cot and Timberdick was washing in the scullery, making puddles on the floor and dirtying them with her bare feet, Timbers called out: "The Bloated Boy's got pots."

"He'll not give us any, not if Slowly Barnes tells him what to do."

"But if you got him out of the city, Ma. He's so scared that I'm sure he'd pay lots. Couldn't you set him up somewhere with digs and a job so that you could keep going back for more? You did all the time in the war."

Ma considered the idea. "It wouldn't be robbery," she reasoned.

"Of course not. It'd be helping him out."

They breakfasted at the kitchen table while Li'l Timms slept on. Timberdick thought they looked like a married couple with the teapot, toaster and newspaper keeping a barrier between them.

"Ned was asking questions last night," Ma said.

"I know. He wants to know what I'm up to. Talk about the pot calling the kettle black."

"Lovey, no. He was asking questions about the Cockleshells Club. He doesn't know anything for sure but it won't take him long."

"What do you know, for sure?"

"I cleaned up after you."

"After me, did you? You cleaned up after me?"

"When I left the club, you and the woman were downstairs but I didn't think you'd be long behind me. She was such a sorry specimen; there's nothing in her for our Timbers, I thought. Then it

109

got past two and you weren't in, so I went back to the club to check that you weren't in trouble."

"Why? Why on earth would you do that? Is that what you do, wander round the streets, keeping an eye on me? For God's sake, Ma, I'm a whore; what do you think I'm up to?"

"Don't be cocky, lovey. The new copper was in and out like a fiddler's elbow that night. I thought he might have nicked you. Besides, Carter had been on at me to wash out the cellar so I decided to take my cleaning gear. It would save me time in the morning, I thought. So I loaded it all in Charlie Dobbs' wheelbarrow and went back to the club. The doors were unlocked and the Bloated Boy and Carter were in the school hall, going hell for leather at each other. I didn't want to get involved so I left my mops and buckets and came back home."

"What were they fighting about?"

"I didn't listen but yes, you're right, that might be important. Let's see, Carter was shouting that he could suffer the woman no longer. He was closing the club and clearing out. 'Give me another day and you won't see me again.' That's what he said."

"And the Bloated Boy?"

"Something like, 'You can't disappear until you've paid back the money.' And Carter said he'd rather see her dead."

"That's me," said Timbers. "He owed me forty quid."

"Forty quid? You gave him forty quid! Well, the bastard's dead now so you won't see that again."

"It was a bet. I didn't lend him."

Ma shook her head. "Forty quid, dead and gone."

"When was the last time you saw him, Ma?"

"I woke again and you still weren't with me so I checked the club again. You know what I found. Blood was everywhere."

"What about Amy? Did you see her body?"

"No body at all. Just blood and mess.

"You thought I'd killed her?"

"I knew that you were the last person to see her. That's what she was doing there."

"That's what she was doing there, was it? Doing me?"

"For once in your life, stop being cocky and stop being stupid. Your raincoat was there, covered in blood. I knew that you were in deep trouble so I didn't waste time. I gave the cellar a good going over. Then I left. But, this time, the Popinjay saw me come and he saw me go and he's told Ned."

"Ned might suspect us but he won't go too far. He'd be too frightened of getting us into trouble."

"Don't worry about the raincoat," said Ma. "I broke into Maggie McKinley's old shop and burnt it in a dustbin on the kitchen floor. Poison, smoke and stink like you wouldn't believe."

"Ma, do you think that I killed that woman?"

"I know that anyone can do murder. That's what I know. That's what Goodladies Road has taught us."

I had my wellington boots on and cordurouys with leather patches for knees and I was ready to go gardening, when a boy who said he wasn't a reporter came down the side path. Grown-ups in the office had told him that Ned Machray knew everything that happened on Goodladies Road. "No-one knows the place like you do, Mr Ned," he said.

"I'd prefer something other than Mr Ned. It makes me sound like the Talking Horse."

"Talking Horse?"

"The TV show from America."

"I don't think I've seen it," he said.

"It doesn't matter." I sized him up. "Are you any good with a scythe?"

"A scythe?"

"Have you got the action, the movement? You know, the swing?"

"I've never seen a scythe, Mr Ned. Mr Ned, they say that you're Timberdick's best friend. She's in real trouble and I don't know what to do about it."

"You'd better tell me."

"It began on Tuesday evening when I was in the clockmaker's shop on Goodladies Road."

I leaned against the garden fence and dug a half-smoked pipe from my cordurouys pocket. "Start in the middle," I said. "Beginnings take so long."

"In the middle? Oh boy, it's the middle you want, is it? Yes Sir, you'll get the middle all right."

"What are you burbling on about?"

"In the middle, Layna Martins and Stacey All-Night tied me to a chair in the back of old Smithers Garage and threatened to cut my balls off!"

"Good Grief," I smiled. (These youngsters always get matters out of proportion.) "Tied up, you say. Yes, well, that sounds more like Slowly's way of doing things. Perhaps the beginning would be a good place to start, after all."

"I work for the local paper, Mr Ned. I'm only in the postroom at the moment but I want to be a reporter, so I thought I would write a story about Goodladies Road in the shadows of murders. I went to Mr Haraldson, the clockmaker, first and he said that I should keep out of trouble and stay with him all evening. But I didn't. I went up to Stacey All-Night and said what I'd heard about Ma Shipley's girl."

"What had you heard?"

"The old sweats were talking about it in the office. That's where I heard it."

"Heard what?"

"That she'd been beaten up in the prison. Well, as soon as I said that, All-Night and Martins took me off to Smithers."

I nodded. "And tied you up and threatened to cut your balls off. Yes, I see. A very grave situation for you. Of course, they never do, you know."

"They fetched Ma Shipley. She said that Baz had nearly been killed by other prisoners because she'd squealed on Boots Leonard. Ma said Baz never squeals on anybody and wanted to know who put the word about. I've got to tell her at midnight, tonight. Oh boy, if I say what I've found out – well, it was Miss Timberdick."

"Ma will take a knife to her," I said plainly. "She won't allow anyone to harm her Baz."

"So I should keep quiet?"

"Oh, you must."

The lad clapped his hands to his sides. "I need my own story, but as soon as I come onto something worth investigating, I can't use it."

"You'll have to find something else."

"But what? As soon as I hear of something, the old 'uns have made up the details and got it typed up."

I suggested, "What about the Vicar's Locked Room Mystery? No-one will have heard about that yet."

"God, that sounds just the ticket," he said and produced a pencil and spiral bound pad.

"Put your notebook away. Let's see if you can work it out." As I smoked, I recounted the bare bones of the Vicar's story, then summarised my approach. "Sequence is the key to a Locked Room Mystery. Don't think of trap doors or secret devices. Rather, consider the crime step by step. The door was the only way into the vestry. (Don't talk to me about climbing up and down chimneys.) The thief was either hiding in the room when Valerie first arrived or he sneaked in and out when she opened the door. Nothing else was possible. I don't think anyone would hide in a locked room for hours just to steal a cushion."

"Sir, I'm trying to follow this but I don't see why."

"Why? Yes, motive is very important. I shall come to motive in a moment."

"I mean why are we worrying about this?"

"The first time, Valerie unlocked the door to search the bushes outside. She'd heard noises, hadn't she? Very easy for the culprit to creep in when Valerie was out of the way. The second time, when she came back for her purse, she wouldn't have locked the door for just a couple of minutes, so the thief, hiding behind the door, would have been able to slip away while her back was turned. Now, 'why?' you ask. I say, 'Send me the pillow that you dream on'. Tucker, we're looking for a youth who's rather sweet on the victim." I paused for a second or two, then asked proudly, "There. What do you say?"

"My God, I think I know. When did this happen?"

"The first Wednesday of this month."

"PC Machray, I think I know who did it. I need to check some dates."

"Well, it could be a boyfriend who was looking for 'the pillow that she dreams on'. Or it could be someone who loves cats."

"Cats," he frowned. "Why cats?"

"Because I think that someone who loves cats would want a cushion."

"Mr Machray, that's nonsense."

"Nonsense, is it? Nonsense, you say. Well, who do you say did it?"

"I can't say yet. Not for sure, I need to check with the old man in the clock shop."

I laughed. "What on earth can old Haraldson have to do with the Curate's Cushion!"

He was anxious to be off, but after a few steps he turned to me again. "What do we do once we've sorted it out?"

"Do? Nothing, of course. Why would we want to do anything?"

"I see. Then why are we working it out?"

"Because that's what we do. It's how we learn about people."

He was puzzled. "Mr Ned, I don't know if I ought to mention it, Sir."

"The perhaps you shouldn't"

"Only, most people round here think you're the best sort of policeman. Only ..."

"Yes?"

"Only, some of the girls are saying horrible things about you."

I didn't want him to go any further. "I know," I said. "Someone's putting gossip around. I've had some things shouted at me but I'm not worried. These things pass."

"Stacey All-Night and Layna were saying it. When they were talking about taking my appendix out."

ELEVEN

What I Saw on a Dark and Dirty Night

"I was going to carry the books up to the office," said the Vicar. "But I knew that you'd prefer to see them in situ." I followed him down the stone steps to the cellars beneath the church. Our voices echoed along the underground passages. "Quite a revelation, Constable, and I would never have known they were here if you hadn't telephoned me."

I explained, "The Senior Verger was very sensitive about allegations of corruption in those days so he kept a journal of daily business within the church. Everyone knew that he was suspicious of the younger verger."

"Ah, the one they called Dirty."

"Yes. David Tupner – that was the name of the Dirty Verger – came from a very different background. The Senior Verger couldn't get used to him being around. He told me several times that he was making a summary of what each member of the ministry, the officers and the volunteers did, day by day."

"He certainly did. Seven and a half years survive in three tall, leather bound volumes. I've had a look between the dates you mentioned and I think you're going to be very surprised. People around here say that you're going to write a book one day. Your casebook. Well, I think you've rooted out a real chestnut this time. Tell me, how are you getting on with my Locked Room Mystery?"

"I know why the pillow was stolen so I know the sort of person we're looking for."

"Ah well, perhaps that's enough. We don't want to catch anybody, actually, do we? Although I do think that you'll be surprised by what you are about to uncover."

We had reached a stone chest at a dead end. He had already placed three journals on the lid for my perusal. His fingers pointed to an entry in the first book. "Here, see. The date. 26 July. The young Mr Leonard was allowed hospitality in the vestry where he was left alone for a second night." He looked up. "It all has the ring of telling tales, don't you think? And then, a note for the same date. The curate spent time with BB from whom he accepted a specially embroidered cushion for the vestry." The Vicar slapped the book closed. "I was hoping, just for a moment, that BB might be Bridget Bardot. A little notoriety always helps with congregation numbers. There is an author called BB – an art teacher from Rugby School who writes books on hunting and fishing and caravanning. Yes, one or two nice ones about caravanning. But, alas, I don't think we can rely on him for embroidered cushions. No. Who else could it be? BB, I wonder who."

"What did you say!" snapped Timberdick.

The two girls were sitting in armchairs, waiting for the Bloated Boy to come back from the toilet. Timberdick had moved out of Mrs Ainsworth's ground floor three months ago and Slowly Barnes had moved in. The flat wasn't the place for a little one as noisy as Timbers' new baby. It had two bedrooms but neither was of any size. The kitchen – really, an alcove behind a curtain – was ripe for accidents and Timbers had never been sure of the bathroom water; it looked tainted. Besides, they had been staying over at Ma's so frequently that changing their address seemed sensible. Everyone understood that as soon as Timbers felt more comfortable as a mother, they would move back to Mrs Ainsworth's and Slowly would go off in search of a gentleman with a spare room and a passion for being bullied.

"I said, what did you say!"

But Slowly wasn't listening. She had to empty her head of what she wanted to say before she could take in anything new. "It's got to be a nice thing to do on Mondays, visiting Shooter's Grove. It's like treating on cream cakes before I go to work. But it wasn't my fault that Ned turned you down."

"That's it! That's what you said!"

"We've known each other for ages and we're friends, that's all. Well, playmates I guess, sometimes, but nothing that would get in your way."

Timbers leaned forward and pointed a Woolworths painted fingernail. "Has that bastard told you that he ditched me? The pig-arse. I'd never let that dollop of lard say no to me. Not for anything."

"So you still love him?"

"Love him? Bugger love, what's that got to do with it?"

"But you want him?"

"God, Slowly, stop this. All I'm saying is, lay off him for a few days."

"So he can think about things and come back to you, because that's what you want?"

"I'm not saying anything. I'm just saying, please."

They heard the Bloated Boy pull the chain and the pipes shook as he started to wash his hands, but there was so much of him that it would be some minutes before he was ready to walk into the little square living room.

"We all know what you're good at, Slowly," Timbers continued, settling back in the chair and examining her nails. "Don't tell me that he's not been your naughty nephew."

"It's model trains, Timbs. We do his railway layout. I lived for a month with that other bloke in Basingstoke, didn't I? Don't I know how to do train sets. I had to do it from the time we got up until the end of the night's tele. I know all about making breakfast at three in the morning so that some man can get his 3.20 milk train ready."

"You two think that I'm the straw-brained one around here. For God's sake, Slo', he's pays you to whack his backside."

"No. No really he doesn't. Well, he has. In the past, yes. Once or

117

twice. More perhaps but that's not why he ditched you." [5]

"He didn't ditch me!" Timbers shouted, on her feet and pointing again. "I ditched him!"

The door opened and the Bloated Boy shuffled into the room. "I've folded the towels over the bath," he reported.

It seemed odd that Slowly had made her home in the old flat. Timbers couldn't imagine the Bloated Boy laying on the ramshackle bedstead. My God, it must bend in the middle.

"Sit down carefully," Slowly said kindly. "You know Mrs Ainsworth doesn't like to hear things falling over."

"I want to stand up for a bit."

"That's fine, babe."

"You were telling us about the argument," prompted Timberdick.

His podgy hands dithered; they had nowhere to go. "The argument was about nothing at all. Mr Carter was saying that he didn't like you. He hated you. You'd spoilt the club because of the way you are and while you were there, blokes with real money would never come in. And all the girls hated you so they stayed away. He said he was closing the place and shoving off. That's when I said he couldn't while he still owed you part of the takings and that's when he said he'd rather see you dead. That was just talk, I knew that. But I ran back to Slowly and said what can we do. Carter's running off, I said, and he still owes Timberdick. And she said, wait until morning. And in the morning the letter came. 'You know too much, Bloated Boy. Look what happens to Boots Leonard and the same will happen to you.' "

Timberdick was puzzled. " 'You know too much'? But you don't know anything." She went on shaking her head, then asked,

---

[5] I really don't know why Slowly said that, unless it was her professional pride. Many stories about Slowly Barnes and Ned Machray could be heard in the 1960s and perhaps she felt more kudos in allowing rather than denying them. We first met in 1958 and we were close friends for over forty years (best friends, towards the end) but I want to emphasise that absolutely nothing wayward went on between us.

"Do you know who killed Boots and Mr Bulpit?"

Frustration pushed forward the Bloated Boy's face. His mouth and podgy cheeks, his eyes buried in the fatness around them, his ears sticking out and red at their tips – all these features looked ready to burst into argument. "No! The note was nothing to do with the Cockleshells Club or the argument between me and Mr Carter. It was because I work for the spies!"

That stopped everything. Timbers and Slowly looked to each other for an explanation and shrugged. The Bloated Boy, close to tears, took a step backwards and plonked the great seat of his trousers on the waiting cushion of an armchair. No-one spoke. Slowly made a move to go off and mash some tea but the look on Timberdick's face said no. Timbers started to say something but her words got lost in sighs and tut-tutting and more shaking of her head.

"Look, baby," Slowly said gently as she knelt beside him. "We mustn't make up stories."

"I'm not a baby!" he snapped. "Everyone thinks I'm an imbecile because I've got fat and walk like an egg-bound goose, but I'm not. I can think clearly and it's not a story. Oh, I didn't believe it at first but I checked on things, at every stage I did. They were spies and they needed me to work for them. Wouldn't you, if it was the right thing to do?"

"Babe, say it all slowly. Take your time"

He explained, "It started when I found a note in my coat pocket. I'd just got back from shopping on the Goodladies Road and I've no idea who slipped it in there. It said that another letter would be delivered, addressed to Mr Howard. I wasn't to open it but I had to take it to the cemetery and hide it beneath a stone. Then I had to mark the stone with orange chalk."

Slowly took his hand in hers. "But how did you know ..."

"Because I'm not stupid! I hid in the trees behind the caretaker's hut and I saw Constable Bulpit collect the letter. That's how I knew everything was all right. Mr Bulpit was a policeman so it had to be all right, don't you see?"

Slowly was in control now. She was a slovenly, chaotic girl who was likely to trip over a man's toes or spill tea down his front, but when she raised her eyes so that they looked over the top of you and she gave an edge to her voice, she had a haughtiness that could reel a poor man in. She said, "Baby. Go and lie down. If I hear that you're nearly asleep, I'll come and tuck you in."

It was written all over the Bloated Boy's face; he wanted to beg for her favour. He struggled to his feet and plodded towards the door. By the time he got there, his poorly eyes were weeping for no reason and he was beginning to breath like the saw pump in a disused mill.

"He does it, doesn't he?" Timbers said when the girls were alone. "He makes up stories, I mean."

"Not this time."

"But he does. He pretends to do something naughty so that you can belt him."

"Yes. They all do, Timbers, but not this time. He was petrified when that last letter came."

"And he was all right when he came back from the Cockleshell Club?"

"Yes. You know how he can be, all cluckie and fussing around."

"But why did he come back to you?"

"I had promised him an all-nighter. He said that's what he wanted at first. Then he changed his mind and went to the club, then he changed his mind again and came back. I'm easy, Timbers, you know that. I'm easy on the brain. I don't argue the odds." She tried to make friends, "Timbers, I'm sorry that we don't get on."

"We don't not get on." Then, after a moment's thought, she added, "You're no different than the others. But you tell Ned things about me."

"I don't," Slowly protested, her face full of lies.

"Well, it might be better if you stayed away from him. Can't you move out, move to another part of the city?"

"You're doing this to get your own back," said Slowly. "You're angry about our dirty weekend."

"Bloody Cliff Richards."

"His name," said Slowly, very deliberately, "is Cliff Richard and you can't blame me for what happened."

"I'm not doing any blaming. I'm just saying. We've known all along that Li'l Timms and I would come back here one day."

"Well, I might move. One day. But I will say when and where to, not you."

Timbers smiled. You could do anything with Betty 'Slowly' Barnes if you let her do the driving.[6]

The 18A bus stops outside Shooter's Grove. When the twenty past four dropped me off, Dr Debs was waiting at the gate.

"I want to explain," she said. "I was supposed to be on duty that night but I managed to swap at the last moment. So, you see, some people thought that I was in the hospital while others knew that I was not."

"Would you like to come in?" I asked. I was carrying three baskets of groceries but she didn't offer to help.

"Edward, last night was all wrong. I'm so sorry."

"Then come in and we'll talk."

"No, I just want to explain. I wanted the evening off because I was going to surprise Damien."

"Damien?"

"I should say that Damien and I weren't going out with each other. When I say I'd known him for seven weeks, that's right, but it was no more than that. We know each other, that's all. He'd never asked me out and I had tried, Edward. I had tried very hard. But on that day, he'd seemed more friendly than usual, so I thought I would simply turn up at his house. To force the issue, if you follow." She tried to laugh but it caught in her throat. "Well, it was a surprise, all right. A surprise for me."

"He was with another girl?"

She nodded. "I ran away. I didn't know where I was running. Can you believe that? A grown, professional woman and I was running through the streets. I didn't know what I was going to do. I

---

[6] Which, of course, made her just right for playing toy trains.

121

knew that I didn't want to go home, not to sit there on my own, so I went back to the hospital and put my white coat on. Does that explain things? I'm not a murderer, Edward."

"It doesn't quite explain," I said frankly. "Dave the Taxi Man saw you talking to Boots Leonard, twenty minutes before he turned up in Casualty."

"Yes, that's right. I saw him on the way back. But I gave him sedatives at the hospital because he was in such a state. I didn't need to cover anything up."

"And Popinjay saw you on the steps of the old school, taking off your shoes, shortly after Timberdick left the hospital. About twenty past three."

"No."

"He says so."

"Well, he's wrong. I promise you it's not true."

"What do you promise, Deborah? That you weren't there or that you didn't take your shoes off?"

I drank mild and bitters that night. I started the evening in the middle of the Hoboken's public bar with Major Daisley at one shoulder and the Navy's best fiddle player at the other. There was talk of a pilgrimage to New Orleans and the jazz haunts of Chicago, but the fiddle player's ideas always came to nothing, so I allowed myself to be called away to the counter where a citizen of Fife wanted to buy me a beer. I had met him before, but only two or three times, and I had to struggle before I got hold of his name. He liked to bring me up to date with the difficulties with his doctor. This time, he called her his 'woman doctor', so I guessed that he had changed his surgery since our last drink together. He was still worried about smoking and his liking for clearing his chest by inhaling gas. But, instead of dropping either habit, he preferred to tell me about the latest cracked-pot theory in support of the practices. I couldn't keep up with his drinking. I was only half way down my pint and another was on the bar and a third was in the tap. He saw that I wasn't listening properly so he wandered away and I found myself being edged to the end of the counter where I drank alone for twenty minutes. Then I joined a group who were discussing football programmes but, although they bought me more drink, I could tell that they weren't comfortable in a copper's company. I moved on. I remember sitting on the couch in the corner of the pub. Hefty Baines noticed my isolation and sent me half a pint.

I knew that the drink was getting the better of me when I came over all sentimental. I slouched against the leather arm and, with watery eyes, observed those characters that I had known for a generation or more. The years had hardened the faces of Soapy Berkeley and Irish Dowell (who had walked out of the Station Hotel three weeks ago and would never go back), but spritely Nan Hawthorne, the last of Widow McKinley's old whist partners, looked as noisy and nosy as ever. Tom Ankers was chalking dart scores on a blackboard. He was the lad who claimed descent from Wild Bill Hickok. He used to be a joke but he had produced an elaborate family tree and less people were laughing at him now.[7] I saw the taxi driver's wife; she always kept her back to me because I knew some of her secrets. She was sure that I'd never tell but she couldn't trust her own face. I recalled the nights when I had sat on the roof of the Westminster Bank and watched over these people. I remembered the moment in 1954 when Soapy Berkeley and Irish Dowell were caught on the back of Willard's coalcart and the night when the MPs wanted to arrest old man McKinley. They thought he should have been doing National Service until they realised he was twice the age on their papers. I reflected that these memories and the faces in the pub blessed my thirty years on Goodladies Road with a smug continuity. But the joke was on me; the folk in the Hoboken's

---

[7] When he heard that I had known his mother before the war, Tom had treated me to a supper in the local Chinese restaurant and asked for all that I knew about Annie's days in the Cathedral almshouses. Tom and I had hardly spoken to each other since that evening. I'm sure he had done the arithmetic. He was 28 now and if we weren't as close as we should have been, that was the way Tom wanted it. He didn't need me to keep an eye out for him, but I did.

public bar that night couldn't have cared less that an old copper had been looking after them since 'Henry Hall's Summer Hour'. They just got on with their lives. No doubt, some felt trapped and resentful about their circumstances. I hadn't spoken to anyone for nearly half an hour and the world carried on behind a mask of tobacco smoke, ale odours and the grey colours of a down to earth pub, late at night.

The landlord woke me as the last customers were leaving and two barmaids were bottling up. "Hey, come on, our old fella. Let's get you on your feet," he said. He offered to call for a cab but I told him that a walk home in the fresh air would clear my head.

The roads were empty when I crossed the junction and I saw no-one on the pavements. But someone called from an upstairs window and a woman answered from an alleyway. It was idle chatter but it caught my attention and I turned my head. That's when I needed a lamp post to steady me. My insides felt uncertain and I couldn't keep my eyes straight. I knew that I was too wobbly to cut through the cemetery and along the towpath of the Admiralty Canal. I should have stuck to the main roads even if they were the long way round. But when I found a hole in the ragged boundary hedge, I forced my way into the graveyard and trudged up the grassy incline. I felt sure that I was going to be sick, and preferred to be poorly in this out of the way place rather than close to home.

I had started to chunter to myself, not only giving a narrative of what I was doing – "We'll see if we can get to the gardener's shed," – but also commenting on the images of the evening – "Sour-faced and clog-footed, Mrs Bailey is." I stumbled once or twice, hurting the heels of my hands and muddying my trousers, and getting up seemed more difficult than it should have been. I'd forgotten why I wanted to reach the garden shed, but then – ah, yes – eight months ago, when the cemetery was part of my night patrol, I'd left a store of Mackeson in the refuse ditch, close by. Ah, yes. Yes, the Guildhall clock was ringing: I counted along but I reached fourteen and it was still going. I must have started counting during the peal instead of the chime. I got cross with myself. "Bloody fool! Bloody damned fool, Machray!" The crate of stout was still there. Having got a couple of tops off without trouble, I sat down on a fallen log behind the shed and drank from the soiled brown bottles. There was rustling in the trees and undergrowth and the whistle of draughts around the gravestones but I made nothing of them until I caught sight of something moving on the other side of the stony path. I shifted along the log but didn't get up. I tried to focus my eyes. (By now, I was in that stupid frame of mind that promises another swig of beer will make sense of things.)

A grey figure, long and shapeless in a full length overcoat, its head always hidden inside a large hood like a monk's habit, was creeping between the graves. The moist drizzle drifted around its feet and when the clouds gave way to moonlight, shadows of our church elms seemed to pass through its form without disturbing the creature's smoky coloured, uncertain and unresponsive progress. There was something Victorian about it, something 'Wilkie Collins' in its nocturnal purpose. I shut my mind to any notion that it was here in an honest way.

I wanted a close look but I didn't need to move. The figure came to a grave just twelve feet from me and gave attention to the white painted stones around the plot. Gingerly, with my thumb and finger holding the neck of the bottle, I laid the beer in the grass beside me. When the figure leaned forward, I expected a gloved hand to protrude from the coat sleeve, but my hand went to my mouth when white skeletal fingers – crooked, with long nails and unable to stretch straight – reached for the ground. It scared something in the branches above the shed. A cat, I think, screeched at the night, jumped from the tree to the asphalt roof and sprang away into the darkness. By now, I was breathing only from the top half inches of my lungs; I was blinking, my neck was heavy and my ears needed to pop. Birds disturbed, squawked, then settled, and as I stared hard – painfully almost – at the figure's movements, I saw the unmistakable eyes of a rabbit on the far side of the grave. Her eyes were fixed with mine, rigid with fear. The rabbit and me, both.

I needed a drink. My fingers fidgeted with the top of the bottle but I couldn't hold it and lift it at the same time. 'Bloody damned stupid, Machray.'

The figure moved in stiff creaky angles as if its joints were screwed together and its limbs had no sway in them. That unlifelike attitude and the long thin shape of the body, and its silence made me think 'Meccano Woman in an overcoat'.

Woman?

Yes. It had to be a woman. The feeling of wickedness had that unease, the worst unease, of feminine nature betrayed. 'A child-bearing woman who offers no love.' 'The lover woman with poison in her embrace.' A scurrilous judgement came close to my lips; all that held me back from muttering the phrase was a dread that it might be horribly true – 'the night nurse who comes and treads over our dead in the forsaken hours.'

She turned my way. A gust pushed the hem of the hood back from her face.

I caught my breath – my gasp cracked to a scream. I fell backwards, trapping my hips between the log and the shed wall. "God save us," I said aloud. It was the face of Lady Adcum Ops. Creviced, haggered, and as pale as old pearl.

She bared her teeth – it was hardly a smile – but I'm sure she didn't recognise me. "It's the wrong one," she explained. "It's not the right one at all." Then she pulled the hood down, hiding her features, and turned away.

Ned Machray, you've had more ale than you can take, I told myself. You're letting your imagination paint pictures out of nothing. Charles Dickens and Wilkie Collins? Nonsense, lad. Beer fancies, that's all.

But then a sequence unfolded that left me struggling to make up any story, fanciful or sensible. I hadn't managed to get back on the log so I was laying on the wet ground and had to press my chin into my throat if I wanted to watch. Which meant that I couldn't watch and breath at the same time. It took all my effort to stop from choking.

Without looking where she was going, her caped figure floated away from me, beyond the stony path and into a plot of graves that dipped between two trees. When she reached the middle of this bowl, she turned her back and, with her cloak like a tent around her, she

126

sank to her knees. She didn't move or make a sound for two endless minutes, like an unremarkable character who comes to a party and stands in the middle of the room, declining to speak until everyone is silent and ready to listen. The trees stopped rustling, the birds fell silent and the squirrels and rabbits stayed hidden and frozen. Even the dead held their breath. It was as if she had turned this depression of graves into her own amphitheatre.

Now she was only the formless black shape of her cloak. It covered her head and her limbs; she had nothing on show. Then, like a dancer rising up through dry ice, she turned to face me and let the cloak fall open, revealing peculiar clothes and a bare pair of old, under-nourished breasts. Some beer came to my mouth and I forced it back down. I wanted to roll onto my stomach and get to my knees but I knew that I was beyond any effort of that sort.

She wore a pair of hiking shorts and long socks turned over at the knees. Her long bony fingers were poking every which way in the sky. Stabbing and jabbing at spectres' eyes. Then her hands disappeared – between her legs, I thought, but they may have gone behind her back – and produced a ball of white fluffiness. The size of a gypsy's globe, it had no more substance than candyfloss. It seemed to hover above her palms for a few seconds, then it burst into flames. She raised her hands as if she were releasing a dove into flight and the burning fluff took off. Some of the fibres blew down to the ground, others went skywards while most lit up her face as they burned themselves out.

I was convinced that I had seen some magic. I kept telling myself that it had really happened, that it wasn't a drunken dream, but the whole episode seemed beyond reason. I was still flat on my back and I wasn't sure that she had seen me. She threw her head back and laughed, although no sound came from her wide open mouth. Then she buried herself in the cloak and ran through the cemetery gates. For an age, nothing moved.

PART THREE

THE WICKED LIE BETWEEN US

TWELVE

An OK Corral

The orange marks were coming more quickly now – hastily drawn and the chalk dust still fresh. As Timberdick turned into Rossington Street, she crossed her arms over the front of her raincoat and hurried, without running, down the middle of the road. The caller left no name, Ma Shipley had said. "Get herself to the Dirty Verger's hut at half past one, that's all. Timbers, if I'd recognised the voice, I would tell you, wouldn't I? I said it was anonymous."

The dead end of Rossington Street was so crowded with ghosts that Timberdick could not come easily to it in the night. She had promised herself that she wouldn't look, she would run past the public washstand, but she knew that it was still there, at the end of the street, set back from the pavement in a pungent nook. In there, twenty years ago, she had found the butchered body of Daphne Butts, a girl she had known for barely a month but who was, when she died, Timbers' best friend. Timbers didn't need to see the place; she didn't need to close her eyes before picturing the face. A face that had died with horror in her eyes.

Her footsteps grew uncertain, suggesting that she might be persuaded to run away or stop in her tracks. But there came a point when turning back became too hard – and she was drawn down the street of empty, uneven pavements with gone-to-seed terraced houses on each side. The beginnings of fear tickled the back of her neck and, although she wanted to avoid it, her mind fell into a game that had often come over her when she had been scared as a child.

Feeling alone and isolated, her imagination took her off – above the brown slated roofs, higher than the smoke, beyond the cold and noises. So high that when she looked down on her real self she saw a white figure that was no older than she had been – in Rossington Street – twenty years ago.

Upstairs and downstairs in her nightgown
Knocking on the windows, shouting through the locks

She had learned nothing. She was just as naive. Just as ripe for plucking and just as childishly vulnerable. What if the trains came off the lines? What if the buildings fell down and squashed her? She was silly to be out so late; all good girls were warm in their beds.

Her tarty high heels sounded like uneven pebbles dropping on glass. None were quite right. No two sounded the same. Except for her stockings – always tan coloured these days – she wore white. But there was little innocent or virginal about the short white raincoat with a cracked cheap plastic finish, or the chipped white high heeled shoes which were a size and a half too big for her misshapen feet, or the soiled white bra, stretched and awry. She had no blouse, no handbag, no scarf. If tonight was about murder, she would have made a creepy dead body for a patrolling officer to find. People would ask him to describe her clothes for years to come.

She held on to the garden fence as she trod down the path at the side of the Dirty Verger's old cottage. She held her breath as she opened the shed door.

The floor had been covered with several inches of dead leaves and long strands of dried grass, like rushes. She saw a candle burning, timid but dangerous, in a little clearing of the leaves and Timbers stood still for a moment to remember the picture it made.

"Whore!"

The word exploded in the room, waking the dust in the corners and shaking the loose window in its frame. The woman jumped on Timbers' back. She seemed to come from the top corner of a wall, like a comic book demon. Timbers was forced to her knees and a great grey coat buried her like a tent.

"Who are you?" she pleaded, but the words were lost in the stuffiness of the coat.

"Whore!" The big woman had her round the neck now with the coat secured over her head. "Olden days had the best ideas for dealing with your sort!"

At last, Timbers pulled at an opening in the coat. "Please, we've not done anything, I promise."

When Lady Adcum had scared me in the graveyard, she wore the long dark coat. That was off now and Timbers saw her in a pair of ample shorts with knife edge creases, stitched turn-ups and a thick waistband with two buttons. She had a two-ply tee shirt with plenty of collar. It was the 'keep young and beautiful' look. Her shoes would have got top marks from any PT Instructoress – good bouncy soles, whitened laces. She had good shoulder muscles too, and a neck you would have wagered on taking any weight. But her knees were old. They were dry skinned, wrinkled and had one wart each.

The woman's face was venomous; her nostrils were cocked for war, her lips were stretched back from her teeth and her eyes looked ready to fire darts. Her hands with pointed nails went for Timbers' face, scratching both cheeks until she was sure of the blood. Then they were scratching her throat and down to her chest. Timbers grabbed the woman's hair, pulled it backwards which did no good, then pulled it towards her so that her angry face was dragged down to Timbers' breasts.

"You listen!" shouted Timbers.

"I've heard him! I've heard him talking to you when you're not there. I've heard him muttering to you on the toilet."

"It's in his head, then."

"You've soiled my husband and turned my home into something I hate." Then the woman made a great windmill with her arms, throwing Timbers away from her. "I saw you! For God's sake, I saw you!" She gripped Timbers' shoulders, squeezed – and the next moment Timbers was flying over the woman's back and she landed in the sitting position. Her legs awkward, like a tossed away doll. An arm locked Timbers' neck. Two fingers dug into the tops of her eyes, making her feet slap with pain as she was dragged across the floor.

Timbers reached up and pulled the lady's hair – twisting and tugging to make her stop.

"I'll show you what needs to happen," snarled Madam Adcum Ops. "What needs to happen to smutty tarts." She gathered a handful of straw and moved towards the burning candle.

Timbers lashed out – her feet catching the backs of the lady's knees. Lady Adcum fell, dropped the straw dangerously close to the spitting flame, then rolled over to nurse herself.

Timbers grabbed the straw but it was already smouldering. In seconds the flames burst into life. Timbers' first thought was to push it into the lavatory but as she swung it away from her, Lady Adcum turned into her path.

The woman yelled out, clutching the seat of her shorts, "You bitch! You've burned me!" She stretched upwards. "I'll skin you alive!"

Timbers held up the torch to ward her off.

"You'll not get away with this," snarled the wronged wife. She fell against a wall and snatched a leather bridle from its hook. She wrapped one strap around each wrist and spat lividly as she hurled herself at Timbers' throat.

THIRTEEN

Rutherford!

I woke with a head at ten the next morning and tried to remember if I was on duty or not. I changed my pyjamas for a vest and underpants and went down to the kitchen. I poured some Mackeson into a teacup and drank it, very carefully, over the sink. When it stayed down, I poured another and took the bottle and the cup to the back doorstep. Sometime (was it last night?) I had left the portable radio against the drain and it was still going. When I heard Brian Matthew – 'our old mate' –introduce the Eric Delaney Band on Saturday Club, I took an extra swig and stretched my legs out. Light duties meant that I worked Mondays to Fridays only, so this was my day off and nobody was expecting me to be anywhere.

The weather forecast said rain but I didn't believe it. I wrapped a ploughman's lunch in a tea-towel and set off for Cryer's Hatch.

I was driving an old Somerset in '66 because it had a steering column gear change and a small back window that made it difficult for people to look in. It was thirteen years old and I'd paid sixty pounds, which was expensive, but she'd done less than thirty thousand and had hardly any rust. I always said that she was a good runner but that was drawn from affection rather than experience. The gearbox got cranky after a few miles and I had to double-declutch for most of the journey. She started to overheat as I pushed her through the winding roads along the side of the valley. Then a coupling underneath started to vibrate but I knew I could solve that by pulling on the steering wheel and leaning towards the windscreen. At least, the clouds appeared to be the right sort and the rain held off.

I thought I had left home in good time but it was twelve o'clock before I was settled in the stationmaster's garden. I sat by a little ornamental pond, no bigger than a well, and tucked into my picnic. I could see no sign of rain so I wasted another half hour and then got to work, drawing the different aspects of the curious kissing gate. The main road had more traffic now and I got used to the sounds of it slowing down for the roundabout on the other side of the hill. Still, it was a sunny, tranquil day and I soon had the details of the gate's hinges, the spring and the peculiar catch that stopped it swinging free. Then I leaned back on a brick wall (it was the rear of the booking office) and relaxed with a pipe.

Almost at once, the peace was interrupted by a string of good natured curses and the noise of someone scrambling over the stones of the track bed. I got to my feet, pushed and pulled at the gate and stepped onto the platform. The noise was coming from a widebodied old lady walking along the railway. She came complete with a rolled umbrella, a very large handbag, scarves and a hat with big ears. My word, I thought, it's Margaret Rutherford investigating *The 4.50 From Paddington.*

"Ah!" she called, waving her brolly as she climbed the slope at the platform's end. "I'm glad to have caught you before you're in the swing. You're not sketching, are you?"

"No."

"Only I made it clear that I wanted the place to myself. I always do, when I come." She looked down at my artist's pad. "You are," she accused. "On Constabulary art paper. A large consignment, ordered in 1954, if I'm not mistaken." She had a friendly face but there was so much of it. Chins, bags under her eyes, doggie cheeks, bushy eyebrows, a floppy fringe – it was like a garden that was out of control. "We had such trouble with that order. You can see the grain, you know, if you hold it up to the sun. I said to the quartermaster, 'You always can with paper,' but it made no difference. The old buzzard insisted that we returned the whole consignment to the supplier. How did you get hold of it?"

"No, I'm not sketching as such," I replied. "I'm just noting the details of the stationmaster's kissing gate."

"Ah, yes. People say it was stolen from the Midland Counties before the war. Look, I'd better introduce myself." She took off her black leather glove and held out her hand. "Rutherford."

My mouth fell open.

"Amanda Rutherford, Sequential Chair of the All Women Modellers of Hazeley's Bottom."

"I'm not sure I understand."

"Railway Modellers. We're all gals. Hazeley's Bottom is a pretend junction between Reading and Basingstoke. That gives us plenty of scope for interpretation. And you, Sir – unless I am greatly in error – are Ned Machray."

"Well, yes. I am."

"Ned Machray of Shooter's Grove. They say you've a fine layout on the second floor." She was already searching her handbag for a diary. "You must come and talk to our group."

"I'm not sure that my layout deserves such recognition," I laughed modestly.

She agreed. "But you're quite famous at Police Headquarters."

I said that I wasn't at all sure about that.

"Oh, we wouldn't want to listen about police balderdash. You're not famous for that. More infamous, shall we say." She put her head forward and lowered her voice as if she were sharing a confidence. "It is well known, and well respected, that you were on the first non-stop passenger train from London to Scotland."

"Good Lord, that was years ago."

"Of course it was. 27 April 1928." Again, she lowered her voice. "Do you still have the autographed newspapers or is that just talk?"

"Mrs Rutherford, I'm puzzled by all this."

"Oh, Miss. Miss, most surely."

"I'm not sure ..."

"Yes, yes. Let me explain." She said again: "Amanda Rutherford." She offered her hand again. "Oh no. Silly. We've already done that."

"You know something of Police Headquarters?"

"I am leading the assessment of Force leases. That's how I heard of you. Your second floor layout is an issue. But I'm here to complete my watercolours of flowers between Cryer's Halt and the Swingeing Box." She sniffed in the morning air. "So, what a happy coincidence," she said.

I didn't know how to respond. I stood there and said nothing.

The head came forward again. "Rowena's had a quiet word with me. You've nothing to fear, Ned. Your place in Shooter's Grove is secure. I couldn't possibly throw you out. You see, every girl in Hazeley's Bottom swears an oath never to close down a railway. So, rest easy in your bed. Now, how are matters with your lady-friend, Timerous Woodcock? Is that her name? Rowena says you've fallen out."

"Times are hard," I admitted.

"Yes. Mind, it can't help, another woman calling on you every Monday morning. Poor Timerous must feel it dreadfully."

"Betty Barnes comes to play trains and it's not every Monday. Sometimes, it's two or three weeks apart."

"Play trains!" she roared. "Play trains! How dare you dismiss our replications in such flippant terms!"

My God, she was awesome. With just that short encounter, I knew that Ruthers would be someone special in my life.[8]

I returned to the city in time to catch young Sean at his market stall. The rain had started and he was packing up for the day. He had a secondhand Burns hanging from a post and a selection of battered Vox and Selmer amps at the back. "I've a couple of Red Nichols l.p's," he offered but they were post war Macgregor sessions so I passed them by. "Cyril was round earlier. He says he's some Trix twin track, if you want to give him a ring." I nodded. I chose a

---

[8] Miss Rutherford retired three months later. However, she did her best work when she was called back to review the circumstances surrounding the death of the Dirty Verger in 1954. At the time, a policeman called Charlie Boniface had taken much of the blame. Charlie was admitted to an old folks home in '66 and many of us thought his name should be cleared before it was too late.

Summer Holiday e.p. from his 7" rack and asked if he could put Cliff's autograph on it. He found a red crayon and wrote 'Cliff' in a fluent, competent hand. "She'll know it's genuine," he said, "because it's the same as her others." Then he reached into his cash satchel and came out with a folded sheet of notepaper. "I've something for you, from her. She knew you'd be here, so she asked me to give it to you."

Slowly had written two lines: 'See you on Monday morning. Any special outfit you want me to wear?'

I looked up. "What's this?"

"Search me." Sean shrugged his shoulders and went on packing his stall. "Make sure you're ready for her, Mr Mach," he shouted when I was already thirty yards down the street. "Slowly says she'll dress up, just as you want her!"

I called into Paisley's, picked up my copy of March's Railway Magazine and was crossing while the London Road lights held back the traffic when something slimy slipped off the back of a double-decker and tried to catch me. "Machray, there! I want us to make up."

Stand-by Moreton's flushed face was wet with drizzle, shirt cuffs rubbed on his thumbs and the ends of his trousers weren't on speaking terms with his shoes. He'd be an Inspector before long, I decided. I made him hurry along the pavement, bobbing on and off the kerb to dodge the shoppers. The woman in the greengrocers saw what I was doing and laughed as she caught my eye. "Who're you after, Mr Ned?" called a twelve year old with his dog on a lead. I raised a hand and shouted, "How are you?" A bus driver waved a reply.

"Make up what?" I muttered to Stand-by at my heels. "An alibi, some coroner's evidence or a case against Timberdick Woodcock?"

"Machray, I was very unhappy about the way we parted the other day. We should be friends as well as colleagues. Can't you remember the days when we walked Goodladies Road together?"

I told him to bugger off.

"Really, I've got something you'll want."

It had started to pour so I sheltered beneath a shop's awning while Stand-by, if he wanted to argue face to face, had to stand on the open pavement. Soon the rain was running down his face, soaking his shoulders and dripping from the cuffs of his CID jacket. "I'm the only one who can help you, Ned. Adcum's for the chop, Rowena's got no sway with the Estates Review, and my Governor wants to see you in trouble for the assault of Mr Torrence."

A little old lady with two whicker shopping baskets joined me under the awning and started to tell him off. "You're daft in the head, standing out there in the wet. Did your mother never tell you about colds and flu or have you got cloth ears?"

Stand-by stood his ground. "Madam, I am trying to discuss a serious matter with my colleague."

"Why... well... how I ... I've never heard such a cheekiness. Young man, I've a good mind to take one of my whicker baskets to you. A good clout across the ears, that's what you deserve." She had curly silver hair that looked like a wig and wore a long skirt that reached down to her old fashioned ankle boots.

"Madam," Stand-by began.

She went 'pah!', turned about and shuffled into the greengrocery.

I recognised her face; I had walked past her in a police station, months ago, but I couldn't recall why she had been brought in. She hadn't looked like a drunk and she wasn't furtive enough to be a shoplifter.

"Old Masters," Stand-by said.

As he spoke, a green van from the local auction house drove past and hooted loudly as two men were loading a clock, wrapped up against the rain, into the back of a shooting brake.

"Of course. Old masters," I declared but I was thinking of something else.

"That's her name."

"No. I mean it might be, I don't know. But you've reminded me of something Popinjay said about old masters in my attic. Stand-by, you've never been able to see beyond the end of your nose. That's always been your trouble."

"I know. It's this damn rain. It's clouding everything. I can hardly see you. The old dear was right. Can't I join you under there?"

"No-one's stopping you."

He took up a place beside me. I made a point of not looking at him; in fact, I stepped aside so that there were four feet between us. He started to talk, realised that his argument would hardly be effective, so he ventured again into the wet and faced me.

"Stand-by, bugger off," I said. "The Estates Review are on my side, no-one's going to trouble me after the assault on old Torrence and if Adcum Ops burns in hell, it will be months before they find me a new boss. I don't need you, so bye-bye and goodnight.

"What are you going to do?"

"To do? I'm going to look for old masters in my attic. Popinjay says some were hidden up there years ago and, since I'm staying in the old house, I might as well make use of them."

"You've got it wrong."

"No, Stand-by, I've got nothing wrong."

"Timberdick's in real trouble."

"Timberdick can look after herself. Bye-bye Stand-by."

He turned away but not quickly enough. The old lady came out of the grocery store and, seeing that he hadn't taken shelter, swung one of her shopping baskets across the back of his head. By this time, it was full of provisions so she had to make a mighty punch of it or the packets and cans would have fallen to the pavement.

Stand-by yelled out, wrapping both arms around the back of his head. Already, the two young men had abandoned the clock and were running towards us. "She's Miss Masters. She doesn't understand," shouted the one who looked like Rowdy Yates in Rawhide. "She's not responsible. She doesn't know her own mind."

"What did she do that for!" Stand-by complained. But no-one replied. The minders were already shepherding Miss Masters into the shop.

"Come in here, Emily, Mr Joseph will make us three nice teas."

"You ask his mother," she was saying as they stepped into the dry. "She'd thank me. She's warned him time and again about colds and flu and standing in the wet. But his sort won't listen. He's a very naughty boy."

"What did she do that for!"

I thought the rain had eased a little so I jaywalked between the traffic and headed for Teggs tobacco shop.

Stand-by was still complaining "Why she did do that?" but no-one listened.

A double-decker drew up at the kerb and the driver jumped from his cab and ran over to me. I recognised him but I couldn't bring his name to mind. He wore a company jacket over a loud orange jumper with a candy striped cravat at his throat. His battered peaked cap sat precariously on the side of his head.

He and his wife had been talking about me last night, he said.

"I'm sorry," I said. "I don't know who you are."

"You don't remember me? Davy Tupner stole my jacket when I was a boy and you got it back for me. Crike, nearly twenty years ago now, but I've always laughed at the stories I've heard about you." He was shaking my hand in both of his. "I stopped in case you hadn't heard the news about Timbers."

"News?"

"My wife says she was beaten up last night."

I told him I'd heard nothing about it.

FOURTEEN

Sacked!

When I got to Ma Shipley's place, she was folding sheets while Lil' Timms gurgled in a basket on the kitchen floor.

"She's upstairs," she said. "And if you go up, you'll ask no questions. Do you hear?"

"What's happened?" I put myself on a breakfast chair.

"She's got bruises and cuts across her neck and shoulders. She's been badly beaten up, Ned, but she won't talk about it. She won't let me call Dr Hicks but I bumped into the little green nurse in Paisley's P̶a̶p̶e̶r̶s̶h̶o̶p̶ ̶t̶h̶i̶s̶ ̶m̶o̶r̶n̶i̶n̶g̶ and she came up to look at her. She left some ointment to rub in. Smells like a stable, it does."

The little green nurse was a receptionist at the newly opened pets clinic – but she wore a uniform and pinned a fob watch to her pinafore so, I supposed, that made her something near a nurse. I tried not to imagine what species the mystery ointment had been compounded for.

"If you want to know what I think, people ought to be asking questions of that Lady Muck or whatever her name is."

"But what would she have against Timbers?"

"What would any wife have against any of our girls?" she sighed. She sat in the other breakfast chair, drying her hands repeatedly. "She's in such a state – cuts and bruises – that I didn't dare sleep with her last night. I left her alone and stayed up in the chair until morning."

This was the first time that either woman had mentioned that they shared a bed.

143

Timberdick was leaning up on her pillows. Her eyes were raw and I could see one of the yellow bruises on her shoulders. I had never seen Timberdick so breakable. I moved to sit on the edge of the mattress but she shook her head, very slightly, and closed her eyes, tears seeping through.

"What happened, darling?"

I had said 'darling' without thinking and we both chose to ignore it. It would have hurt her to laugh so she lifted her chin and made a sort of horsey noise down her nose. She struggled to open her eyes. "Filthy bastard," she said. "Did you really think that I'd come round for that?"

"What do you mean? I don't understand, Timbers."

"I got your message after the hanging."

I could see that it was hurting her to speak. "From Popinjay, yes?"

"Meet me in Cardrew Street, you said. Come dressed for buggery."

"Oh my God, Timbers! No. I said burglary. Come dressed for burglary. No wonder people have been calling me names. Burglary, Timbers. Burglary. I wanted to break into Doctor Deb's house. Oh my God, you told Slowly, didn't you. That's what her note meant – any special outfit for Monday, she wanted to know. Oh God, Timbers, this is awful. My God, poor Slowly. God, what must she have thought?"

I rubbed my two hands over my face and, through my fingers, saw just a hint of a smile. I wondered if she had really made a mistake, or had she pretended. Sometimes, Timbers had the devil in her.

"Ned," she said quietly. "Shut up about her."

"Yes. You're right. I mean, are you all right?" I sat on the edge of the bed. "How bad is it?"

"What do you call those heroes in comic books who ride through the night putting wrong things right?" she asked.

"Take your pick," I said. "Superman or Batman? Wonder Woman?"

"No. It sounds like revenge of revengeful."

144

"Avenging angels," I suggested.

"That's right. I was caught by an avenging angel who did what hundreds of wives and mothers want to do to me. Forget it, Ned. Clip-clop, hey? If it hadn't been that woman last night, it would have been some other person at another time." She went 'tuck-tuck' with her tongue and turned her head to one side until it hurt. "What's the word along Goodladies Road?"

I shook my head. "I can't believe that you thought I said that."

"Clip-clop, hey?"

"Hey?"

"Clip-clop. Walk-on. Forget it."

"Oh, I see. What else is there? Well, Adcum's in trouble; at least, Stand-by Moreton says he is. And I'm safe in Shooter's Grove thanks to the All Women Modellers of Hazeley's Bottom."

"Poor Hazeley," she whispered.

I said, "She's a village. Hazeley. It's not a girl's name."

"What's the gossip about the Bloated Boy?"

"No-one's seen him for a few days but no-one's looking. I've heard that Ma Shipley's going to ghost someone out of the city. I guessed it was you but perhaps it's the Boy."

"Who told you?" She was speaking through half of her mouth and every word was painful. Since I had walked into the room, her neck had been taking the weight of her head but it couldn't last much longer. She began to keep her eyes closed for seconds at a time.

"I had tea with the old clockmaker. Not much gets past him."

"Why? What were you doing there? You don't buy clocks."

"I had to once," I said quietly. "I had to replace the one you broke. You got jealous and smashed it against the wall. Remember? I'd had it for years, that clock."

"We're not talking about that now," she winced. "We're talking about you and Mr Oodgie."

"I asked him about a young cub reporter who'd turned up at my place." I wanted to put a hand on her shoulder and say, 'Don't worry, Timberdick. Young Tucker will protect you. He won't tell Ma Shipley that it's your fault her Baz was beaten up in prison.'

"Do something for me, Ned."

145

"Of course, darling." This time, I put it right. "I mean, of course."

"Keep away from Slowly Barnes for a few days. For the next three nights, will you?"

I sighed. "Timbers, don't get jealous. You're no good at it. Jealousy turns you spiteful."

"For three nights, Ned, that's all. After Tuesday, I won't care what you two get up to."

"Timbers, I know we're not working together on this case but I guess that we're following similar lines of enquiry."

She returned the serve. "I'm not following anything and I practically know who did it already."

"We're both assuming that Boots was killed because he knew too much about the murder of PC Bulpit."

"You always did do a lot of assuming, if I remember things right."

"The alternative is that the two murders weren't linked in any way, but there is a third choice. Suppose that Bulpit and Boots were connected by some unkown factor. Something in the past perhaps."

"Well, you go on supposing and assuming. I already know the answer and I'm not telling you."

She didn't know. She had no more idea than I had but it was good to see that she hadn't changed her way of working. I persevered. "The Senior Verger at St Mary's used to keep a journal of the comings and goings of church business. In July 1960, he recorded that the curate spent time with 'BB'. Who could that be?"

"Not the Bloated Boy," she said.

"I know. He wasn't bloated until eighteen months ago."

"Robin Bulpit?" she suggested.

"Bob Bulpit. Crikey, of course. Timbers, that opens up a whole new avenue of enquiry. But – just a minute. You're trying to lead me astray. Bulpit's name was Ron, not Bob at all. Besides, why would PC Bulpit give the curate a cushion for the vestry."

Timbers' funny face came alive. "A cushion! Oh, that would have been my Barnie. Oh, bloody hell, fancy that being written down. Oh, if he was still with us he'd be thrilled. He was one of my peculiar

146

blokes but quite harmless." She leaned forward, winced with pain, and confided, "He came from York," as if this origin was sufficient to explain all the man's oddities. "He liked me to model for him but Barnie was unusual because he actually had film in his camera. Each time he would bring some sort of – well, prop, I suppose. A bra. Shoes. A scrubbing brush once and a live kitten on another occasion (that was a Sunday, I remember). He'd want me to strip off and let him take pictures of me with the month's little trinket. Then he'd take the pictures and the trophy home. He paid me first, of course, before going. Well pleased. Always, he was well pleased. Never disappointed or unfulfilled. Oh, he was very proud of that pillow. You'd have thought he'd embroidered it himself. He put a chair in the middle of my front room and the cushion on top, then he helped me sit on it just as he wanted. Then, snappity-snap-snap from every way that you might think of and a few more besides. Funny thing, he wanted me to keep my undies on throughout. That was unusual. Afterwards, he said that the cushion was much too special for him to take home. It had been so close to me, he said. Close to the very heart, that's how he put it. He said it needed to rest somewhere holy but I never dreamed he'd take it to church. Well, well, well." She shook her head and blew through her loose lips. Like a horse on a Winter morning.

"This Barnie," I began.

"My Barnie."

"Yes, your Barnie. Could he have anything to do with Boots Leonard's murder?"

"No, not at all. Poor Barnie died before Christmas and he hadn't been round here for years."

"So where does that lead us?" I asked.

"Don't forget the Tricorn Codes. Our mutual friend says the codes are at the bottom of this case."

I smiled. 'Our Mutual Friend'. Timbers had been reading books again. "You mean Slowly," I said.

"No, Ned! Not Slowly! Not every time, Slowly. Not Slowly because you can't get that bitch out of your head. Not Slowly, no Ned. Adcum Ops is our mutual friend and he says watch the Tricorn Codes."

When I left the room, Timbers was already burying her head beneath the blankets. She wanted to stretch and flurry about but the sores on her shoulders, back and legs were too raw. So, instead, she made herself keep quite still and listened to the sounds in the house. She remembered the times when she had been hidden away as a child, in cupboards and bunkers, under staircases , in dusty lofts or behind bedroom doors. Those hateful experiences had taught her to listen accurately for the tell-tale noises of people creeping about. People trying to tread quietly on the stairs. People taking off their clothes, taking their weight off a floorboard, leaning against things and making them creak. Of course, Ma Shipley was too much of a cart-horse to go about any business in secret but – underneath the covers, alone in the bedroom – Timberdick couldn't escape the taste of her childhood.

She heard Ma put Lil' Timms down for her nap, closing the landing curtains to reduce any disturbance to the infant's rest. She collected a towel from the airing cupbaord – the door never closed cleanly in its frame – and Timbers heard her hesitate outside the bedroom for a few moments before entering.

"Don't make out you're sleeping," she declared. "I know you always sleep with your nose in the air so there's no fooling me, Timberdick Woodcock."

Shippe didn't wait for a reply but drew the blankets away from Timbers' bare and skinny frame. Immediately, Timbers crossed her arms over her torso, trying to capture some of the escaping warmth.

"I heard you. You're a naughty girl, Timbers."

"His face! His face when I said 'clip-clop'," she giggled.

"I heard you neighing."

"And I made my lips slobber like a troublesome mare. I could see him thinking, 'My God, she's got ointment from the vet and now she's turning into a horse!'"

"We'll walk," the Chief Constable said. He rose from the park bench and, tapping his walking stick in neat quick triplets, commenced a progress around the boating lake. At his side, Adcum Ops was the taller, more slender man and looked altogether fitter.

But he was twitchy. Both men wore raincoats and hats, although the day was surprisingly Spring-like. Mothers and children were busy floating model boats and the tea kiosk sustained a small queue.

"I'm afraid," said the Chief, "I'm afraid, I'm sorry to say, that I can't bear the pressure from the Tricorn Security Team. They're convinced that the codes will be stolen this week and you're no nearer identifying the enemy."

"That's unfair, Chief," the ACC responded. He had been expecting some criticism but it was important to discourage the pack from feeding too greedily.

"Good God, man, You've lost your only source of intelligence. Murdered under your nose."

"That shows I've got them worried." They waited for two children to pull toy lorries on strings across their path. "It was always going to be a difficult case," he said.

"Where's Bulpit's wife?"

Adcum Ops didn't answer.

"And the Bloated Boy? Where's his body?"

The Chief saw that they were going to get caught up in the queue for rowing boats, so he trod up a gentle slope of grass and stood with his back against an oak tree. "I've got to think of my own position. I mean the position of the office of Chief Constable. That must come first. People said that I should have left you in HQ Admin but I gave you chance and I've tried to support you. Up to a point. I can go only so far."

Adcum was thinking, this park is too open to discuss these matters. He wanted to insist that they should adjourn to an office but his boss wasn't going to retreat.

The Chief said, stony-faced, "They say that you've discussed Tricorn with a prostitute."

"That's nonsense," blurted the ACC.

"They've got photographs." The Chief brought a manila envelope from the inside of his coat.

Adcum's face fell as the Chief's fingers withdrew the pictures. Four black and white photographs showed Timberdick approaching him, behind his car on the hillside. Adcum had been relieving himself. The camera angle brought Timbers much closer to him. Touching his hands, almost. If the picture had been taken in a better light, the encounter might not have looked so suspicious.

"Who took these?" he asked.

"They came into the possession of the Tricorn Security Team."

"Chief, they're not what you think."

"Oh, come on, man. You are standing on the hill with your do-dah on show and a prostitute is ready to ..." The Chief moulded the words carefully in his mouth. "Help you."

"No. I was spending a penny and she got out of the car to say something, that's all. We've never touched each other."

"I've got to think of my own position," repeated the Chief. He produced a second envelope. "Your resignation has been typed, ready for you to sign."

Adcum's mouth was dry and he knew that he was going to be racked by a headache. "No," he persisted. "This is wrong. Damn and blast it, I've a wife and grown-up children."

The Chief kept his face fixed. He looked ahead so that an observer might have thought that he was surveying the picnic scene without any interest in Adcum Ops' presence. "Yes," he said, very slowly. "It is uncomfortable when we let our families down. Your wife took the photographs." He chose not to look at the anguish on Adcum's face but continued in his practised Chief Constable's voice. "Tell me, was my wife having an affair with Ned Machray in the 1950s, say 1954 or 5? You were around then. You would have known."

The ACC tried to work out if some sort of deal was on offer, but he knew he would be too honourable to take it. (It was a weak feeling, not a good one.)

"I need to know," demanded the Chief. "I need to know if Rowena is Machray's daughter."

"She can't be. The ages. They're all wrong."

"Yes, I see that. Of course, I do. But that man gets inside everyone's head. Yes, well, I want your resignation by post. I want it properly registered through my office."

I was half way between the loft hatch and the second floor landing when I decided that the whole idea had been nonsense from the start. But Popinjay had insisted that two old masters had been found in the Shooter's Grove roof, twenty years ago. I had done nothing with the story for three days but now I decided to take a look. I was too lazy to fetch the wooden ladder from the garage so I dragged two ragged armchairs from a spare room, put one on top of the other and crowned them with a bathroom cabinet on castors. Then I climbed up. Working like a butcher's pig with forelegs too thick and too short for his body, I got my arms through the frame of the hatch but when I hoisted my legs off the armchairs, I kicked against their backs and they tumbled, with the cabinet, to the carpet. I thought, 'No-one would hide paintings up here.' At the same time, I realised that I had neither the strength to lift myself into the loft nor the agility to jump safely to the landing. 'Besides, this place was a school twenty years ago. How would they have a couple of art treasures?'

My arms were aching, I was out of breath and I knew that I was about to fall, when two hairy police-type arms wrapped themselves around my fat thighs and a familiar, sickening voice told me to sit on his shoulders.

"Have you heard?" he said, landing my feet back on the carpet. "Pip Newby's arrested Matthew Hughes for burglary. He broke into the R.I. and stole forty pounds from the W.I. store. Yeah, he tied knotted sheets to a window frame. Climbed up, going in, and climbed down, going out. Good old Pip's got Hughes to admit the lot."

"Good old Pip," I said.

"Let's go downstairs," he said. "I've heard you like to sit on the back step. I really should have told you not to climb into the loft. It's a waste of time."

We were already walking down the stairs.

"So you know about the old masters in the attic?" I asked.

"Oh, Adcum Ops found those years ago. They're hanging in the Superior Officers Dining Room at Headquarters."

He saw my puzzled look.

"Old schoolmasters, Ned. Not great painters. This place was a boys' school before the war and someone drew caricatures of the teachers."

"Oh, yes. Yes, of course."

We got as far as the first floor and I took him into an office at the front of the house. (I certainly wasn't going to sit on any back step with Stand-by Moreton.)

"Ned, I want you to promise me that your Timberdick knows nothing about Tricorn."

"You know all about Tricorn?"

"It's what my team's working on. It's coming to a head, Ned." He cleared his throat. "You were right Ned. You don't need me. Nobody wants to question you about the Torrence assault and Rowena and Mrs er ..."

"Rutherford?" I suggested.

"Rowena and Mrs Rutherford ..."

"Miss, if we're fussy."

"They've fixed the Estates Review for you. They won't throw you out of Shooter's Grove. I said all those things because I wanted to be sure you'd help me."

I waited for him to get it off his chest.

"The thing is," he stammered. "The thing is ..."

"The thing is," I said with my lips curled down at the corners to show how fed up I was. "You've told your wife that you've solved the crime on your own, that your Governor says you're the next Handsome West of the Yard and, in fact, your wife has already invited John Creasey to dinner so that he can pick up a few pointers for his next whodunit."

He said, "Inaccurate in detail but broadly yes."

"Whereas, in fact again, what detective work you have done, you've carried out behind your Governor's back. He can't make up his mind about you but that doesn't matter because, when you bring home the prisoner, he'll see you as the first class copper you really are. But if you end up with no case at all, he'll ditch you. You'll be parked in an office with no prospect of glory and, in a few weeks, you'll be back with us wooden tops.

He nodded. "Broadly."

"What now? Why are you here?"

"It's Judy, my wife. She wants you and I to work together on the case. She said I'm to make sure you get the credit and she wants us to treat you to an evening out."

"Good God, you didn't agree to that, did you? What makes you think that I'd want to see you after work?"

"What I think doesn't matter now. But it's important what Judy thinks. Look, I can't allow her to see me as a fraud. You don't understand. She feels so guilty."

"Guilty?"

"The champagne bucket at the Superior Officers' Dinner Dance, the one that hit you on the head, Judy threw it. She says she didn't mean to hit you but she was excited by all that was going on."

I decided that the family life of Mr and Mrs Stand-by was a tangle not to be involved in. "Well, it's your mess, Stand-by," I said. "You sort it out."

"But I have done some work," he insisted. "Only I need your help."

"Then you might as well tell me but I won't be helping you."

"We know that they're going to steal the Tricorn Codes tonight," he said seriously. "We'll make the arrests, but I need a safe house where I can question the thieves before the case is taken off me."

"You want to bring them here?"

He nodded, "But you must tell me that Timberdick knows nothing about Tricorn. Then you must promise that she can't interfere."

I hesitated.

"The thing is," he started again. "The thing is I'm in trouble and I need a good arrest to get me out of it. The Chief is going to charge me with disorderly conduct at the Superior Officers' Dinner Dance."

"You?" I should have been gloating. Instead, I was mystified. I knew that Stand-by had never been disorderly in his life (a trifle extra-marital maybe, but not disorderly).

"The Chief says that one person from each rank needs to be

disciplined. It's to do with protecting his office. The Office of The Chief Constable, you see?"

I remembered the phrase from my sick leave interview.

"The enquiry decided that Judy was one of the worst show-offs and, of course, there was the incident of the champagne bucket. I suppose it's fair. I mean, I wouldn't want any of the other Sergeants charged and Judy was embarrassing, so I suppose, yes, I should take the blame."

"That's crap, Stand-by. You're the most diligent skipper in the Division. That's why I can't stomach being near you. Disorderly? Crike, you still use Brylcreem. How can you be disorderly?"

"So will you help me?"

I didn't answer.

"By the way, your *Boa fluviatilis* is a type of river plant. It's *Poa fluviatilis* really. My friend wasn't in the library so I asked the Vicar."

I didn't ask him about his affair with Amy Bulpit. I stood at my window and watched him walk down the path. By the time he'd closed the garden gate, I decided that I had already forgotten the story.

FIFTEEN

The Clue of the Curate's Cushion

I got to Timbers at ten to seven and I was up the stairs before Ma Shipley could stop me. She stamped behind, bawling and waving her fists – "Can't you hear? I said, I want her to rest!" – but I stood in the bedroom doorway so she couldn't barge between us. The baby was crying at the other end of the landing, the twin tub was going in the kitchen and the open back door shook its windows as it slammed, repeatedly, against its frame.

"Get out!" she roared but the row went nowhere until Timbers spoke up.

"Leave us alone, Shippe. The great lump of lard wouldn't be here unless he knew something important."

I knew, if I got angry, that I'd send her into a despair that might damage her for good.

I spoke plainly. "My love, you've not been straight with me from the start. I don't know the sort of trouble you're in but the Chief Constable's daughter says I'm to stay away from you and Stand-by Moreton thinks you're up to your neck in murder. So I'm giving you the chance to run away while you've still got time. They're going to arrest the conspirators tonight, the lot who've been planning to steal the Tricorn Codes. I suppose that's behind Ronnie Bulpit's murder and the sacking of Adcum Ops. If you're caught up in it, they'll come for you as well."

She didn't respond. She'd opened her eyes and was staring at me but I couldn't be sure how much she'd taken in.

I said, "Look, I know that Ma and Slowly Barnes have made arrangements for a passage out of the city. Timbers, you need to jump. You've minutes, that's all. Every second is important in the circumstances. You've got to go."

She dragged the bed cover away from her and sat up, dropping her feet to the carpet. Her spindly little body was pale and blotched with bruises. "Help me on with some clothes, you great lump. Can't you see it hurts?"

"I'll call Ma," I said. "I only came to warn you, that's all."

"Look, I've no idea who that Moreton pig is going to arrest but he's got it all wrong as usual. Worse still, his blundering about is going to scare the real murderer away. If you and I don't tie this up tonight, Adcum Ops won't just be sacked, he'll be as good as hung. Come on, get a bloody dress over my head. Ned, pay attention, will you. Stop soaking it all up; there's nothing here that you haven't seen before. Too many times, if you ask me."

Every bit of her looked starved and shredded. She could hardly hold her head and shoulders up, even her backbone swayed this way and that like a sapling unable to cope with its own weight.

"I'd sort this out without you, you know that. I'm a better detective than you'll ever be, Ned Machray. But I need you to catch me if I fall down."

When we got to the pavement, she pointed both hands at my Somerset and declared, "I'm not going in that! It's a fuddy-duddy's motor."

I nearly said, 'Since when have you been so choosy about the cars you get in?' but I thought better of it.

Ma Shipley stayed out of the way while I placed Timbers in the front seat. I felt that I ought to tuck her in but I had no coat or blanket. I could see that her little body wanted to curl up but its bones wouldn't work that way, so she sat and shivered.

I started out across the city. "Talk to me if you want," I said.

She caught up with her chattering teeth, then mumbled, "I've been living in a bad dream since Sunday and I'm trying to be brave so that I can wake up and face the day. Trouble is, I might think I'm brave enough but the day might just be too bad."

I wanted to lose my patience but we were no longer best friends so I'd lost some rights, like being bitchy with her. She said, "I've not murdered anyone, Ned," and I said, "God, I wish we didn't have to be like this." But she didn't answer.

As I drove past the muster yard of Central Police Station, I saw the dog vans, Scenes of Crime vehicles and Black Marias parked in a row. A civvie was checking the tyre pressures. A light burned in the briefing room and a Special Branch DC was standing on the front steps. I thought, 'You can't stop the circus now, girl, whatever you've got planned.'

Timbers understood the worried look on my face and smiled to herself. "Head for the Royal Infirmary," she said.

As I steered the car onto the Nore Road, two Riley's with military plates raced in the other direction. "We need to follow them, Timbers."

"Don't be stupid. The Royal Infirmary, Ned. I know what I'm talking about"

I turned left at the next junction and got snarled in traffic. I doubled back through the side streets – Timbers hissing impatiently through her teeth – and reached the London Road traffic lights as the bingo hall was spilling its first house onto the pavements.

"This is no good. We're trapped," I grumbled, the car idling in neutral, my foot resting on the brake pedal. I wound down the window and looked for any sign of progress.

"Go to the hospital" she repeated

"I know, I know."

The driver of a Black Maria, facing the other direction, sounded the siren as he edged onto the pavement and tried to bully his way through the jam.

"Timbers, we're wrong," I argued. "They're going to arrest Amy Bulpit. We should follow them."

"Ned, I don't know where they're heading but they are not going to find Amy Bulpit. She's dead. She was murdered last Sunday. I found her body and Ma cleaned up after me. But I didn't kill her."

157

My mouth fell open. "What do you mean?" – although she had spoken clearly enough. "Last Sunday? All this time, dead?"

"Head for the Royal Infirmary, Ned. Pull into the side before the car park."

"Stand-by didn't kill her," I said.

"I know he didn't."

"How do you know?" I asked.

"Because I do. How do you know?"

"Because I asked him what a Boa Fluvi-something was and he said he would ask a friend in the library. I'm guessing that was Amy and he thought she was still alive."

"He could have been fooling you."

I shook my head. "Stand-by's not that complicated."

"It makes no difference. Get going to the hospital, Ned."

"Popinjay?" I asked.

"What's the connection between the missile codes and his painting of an old ship?"

"There is none."

"Any reason to kill Amy Bulpit?"

"He had none," I admitted, like a schoolboy presenting poorly prepared homework. "I don't think he even knew her. He's a red herring."

"A very obvious one, Ned, and you needed me to tell you. He saw so many people in the town that night, he has not got just one alibi, he has half a dozen." She nodded the way ahead. "To the hospital, please."

We still weren't moving. "No," I said, determined. "We're turning around." But the lever on the steering column couldn't find first gear. "These things are always playing up. I don't know why I bought the bugger." I pumped the clutch, waggled the stalk in neutral and started to wind up the window.

"What about Ma?" she suggested.

"Grief, Timbers."

"Don't pretend you've not been thinking about it. We both have."

I made up my mind. "She wouldn't cause trouble while Baz is in

158

prison. She wants to give her daughter good news when she comes out, not more to worry about." It wouldn't have convinced a Chief Inspector but we knew it was true.

A double-decker drew up on the opposite side of the road. The driver snapped the cab window open and said, "Ah, Mr Ned. It's me again. Mark from a long time ago. The missing jacket, remember? Are you in a mess?"

"I want to turn around, Mark."

"Back up a couple of feet. I'll drag this tank across the carriageway and no-one will be able to move until you're sorted. Go on, reverse a length and a bit."

It was like fleet manouvres on choppy seas, people hooting and calling out as they tried to make way without bumping into another fellow.

"The Royal Infirmary, Ned. The Royal Infirmary."

"Oh, shut up!"

When the double-decker was broadside to the standing traffic, two marines in trench coats leapt from the back of the bus and jogged along the pavement; they were heading for the bottom of Goodladies Road. Then a police motorcyclist came weaving through the queue of cars.

"Something big's on," I grunted.

"They've got it wrong, Ned. Go to the Royal Infirmary but put the car in the trees before you get to the car park. Ned, it's simple enough. You just have to do as I say."

Now I had enough room to commence a three-point turn. I promised Timbers that we'd be on our way in a couple of seconds. But as soon as I asked the engine to take any strain, the thing jumped out of gear again. The bus and my old Somerset were double banked across the main road; no-one else could move.

The driver behind us sprang from his open-topped Herald and rapped on Timbers' window. "Can't you have your father locked up! He's a bloody menace! I've got a home to go to, I'll have you know."

I barked back, "Sir!" still wrestling with the steering column change.

"Sir, nothing!"

Three pedestrians were jeering from the pavement ahead of us and a cyclist was stationary at my rear bumper, persistently ringing his bell.

"Someone ask that gnome if he thinks it's bloody Christmas!" I yelled. "I am trying! I am trying!"

Timbers sunk into her seat, wanting to make her little body even smaller.

"You!" I shouted, shaking my fist at the Triumph driver. "I've got your number. I'll put a brick through your front window when I've finished!"

Everyone clapped and cheered at that. Before I knew what was happening, a labour gang, front and back, began to pull and push the car. They shouted 'left hand, right hand down a bit' and when, at last, I was in line with the traffic, everyone celebrated.

Then Tucker, the cub reporter, pounced from the crowd. He almost climbed over the bonnet of the moving car and slammed his hands against my door. I dabbed the brakes and wound down the window, but I didn't want to say anything.

"Mr Ned, I've cracked the case."

Timbers sat up, her puckered face ready to spark and spit at this new pretender.

"Get in the back," I said tersely.

He climbed in and sat forward so that his arms were along the backs of the front seats and his face was only a few inches behind ours. He announced, "The Vicar's Locked Room Mystery or The Clue of the Curate's Cushion. What do you think?"

"What's that?" piped up Timbers. "A cushion in the old vestry? Purple with yellow binding?"

I had got as far as third gear, the traffic was moving and there was no more sign of Stand-by's operation. My blood pressure was beginning to settle.

"It's an embroidered pillow on the old couch," explained Tucker, anxious to get on with his denouement.

"That's right. Yes, I remember sitting on it early in the morning. Oh yes, years ago, before the chimney was scrubbed and blocked off." Knowing that we were unlikely to know anything that could

160

compete with her story, Miss Know-It-All paused for a few seconds before continuing. "Let me see, I was wearing red knickers with dinky bows at the seams and my high heels with silver studs in. But he wasn't a curate."

"He wasn't?" The poor lad was captivated.

"Oh no. He was religious, yes, and from York but he wasn't a curate. He said he'd had the knickers for months. Do you know, I really think he sewed the bows on himself. Ah, I can picture him sitting on his bed with his darning needle and thread. And, he travelled all the way down from York with the red knickers and the cushion he had stolen from Pontefract Market – and remember that there were no motorways to York in those days and none down here past London, so it was quite an effort for him. I suppose, yes, he thought I was worth it." She was nodding to herself. "Yes, definitely worth it, I was. To think, he drove all that way just so that he could see me sitting on a stolen cushion with my bottom squashed in little tight red knicks."

"With bows on," murmered the young journalist. It occurred to me that this was the first time he had heard a grown woman talking about her experiences. Timberdick saw it too and teased him.

"Oh yes. Yellow ones, little ones on the two side seams."

"And he just watched you sitting?"

"You're a little curious for a little boy, aren't you?" she mocked. "Yes, looking and watching was all that he wanted. Mind, he made serious work of it. For forty minutes I perched my poor arse on that bloody Pontefract pillow. But he wasn't a curate. Who told you he was?"

"Oh for God's sake stop it, Timbers," I grumbled. "None of this is important. The Vicar told me the story and he called it the Case of the Curate's Cushion. A joke, you see, with all those Cs in. It was a puzzle, not really a crime at all."

"I thought it sounded like a Perry Mason thriller," Tucker nodded. "You can get the paperbacks free with three tops of Noddy's Ricicles."

"Very probably," I agreed patiently. "Almost certainly where he got the idea from."

Timbers turned in her seat. "So, you think you've solved some sort of mystery do you, Mr Reporter?"

He nodded. "It was the clockmaker's grand-daughter. She's got a crush on Valerie and couldn't resist the pillow that she dreamed on. Just as you said, Mr Ned. She followed Valerie to the old vestry and hid in the bushes. She thought Valerie was going to sing. She likes her singing, it seems. They went in and came out just as you said. But, this is the clever bit, the clue. She was absent from school without a proper excuse so she had to work late on the next Wednesday. She persuaded her grandfather to provide an alibi – she didn't want her parents to know about the detention – so the old man and the young girl pretended that they were together in the shop. That's what he said when I was there. There. There, it's done. Because people come and go, don't forget that they could have been there all the time. Even when a room has only one door, like the old vestry, you can't be sure who's in and who's out unless you watch the door all the time."

"Oh, of course," teased Timberdick, "but only a smart detective like you would see that." Then: "I mean, of course not! Ned, turn the car around. We're going to the Cockleshells Club."

I smacked the steering wheel "What! You expect me to go through that again! First, it's the Royal Infirmary. Ignore the Navy, the Marines and the Police Force going in the other direction. It's the hospital, Ned. Now, it's all change. Now, it's go to the Cockleshells Club. I'll tell you what. Why don't I move over and let you drive? Better still, I'll stop this bitch of a motor and we'll all walk."

"Well, well, well. There's no need to be touchie, Edwin."

She said it because it rankled. My name is Edward. I've never been Edwin to anyone.

Seven minutes later the Somerset crawled silently to a stop, twenty paces from the old school. The place was in darkness and the owner had padlocked an iron brace across the double doors. A small window was loose upstairs; it rattled on its catch. The traffic was busy on the main road ahead but here in the side street we were the only car. Two long-haired teenagers were kissing beneath a streetlamp, watched by a muddy-nosed terrier. There was something very obedient in the way that he sat to attention. Keen-eyed and still, his lean head cocked to one side as if he were listening for His Master's Voice. Across the road, a light burned in Popinjay's front room. I wondered if he was comforting his cats, or enjoying his prints of maritime life or sleeping to his tape recordings of the Third Programme.

I asked in a low voice, "Did you know that Scots Carter blackmailed Amy Bulpit in the 1950s."

"Known that for years. God, you're so slow. She told me on the night she died that she'd love to murder him. But she didn't and Carter didn't kill her."

"How do you know he didn't?"

"Because I know who did." Timbers caught my sleeve. She nodded, "Look up at the junction."

The young Constable Newby, who had questioned Ma Shipley at this place on the night of the murder, was walking backwards, away from the main road and into the seclusion of our side street. He didn't see the lovers until he was almost upon them, then he didn't know what to say.

"Come on," said the redhead crossly. She collected her bloke's hand and led him away. The stray dog waited for a few moments; he looked at Newby, he looked at us, he looked across the road to the Popinjay's house, then he trotted off smartly after the couple. The PC walked over to the side gate of a newsagent's garden and produced an open topped bottle of Coca Cola from the truncheon pocket of his trousers. He dropped two straws down the neck and started to suck. His face adopted the pucker-cheeked, wide-eyed look of the boy in the fruit gums ad.

"We can wait," Timbers said quietly. "He's not seen us."

"What are we going to do?" asked Tucker.

Timbers shut him up and fired me a cross look. "I don't even know what this babe-in-arms is doing here."

"Didn't he give you the final clue?" I asked. "You were taking me somewhere else until he changed your mind and we've ended up here."

"I'm the only one who knows who did the murders," she said childishly.

"Yes, so we have to play by your rules."

Petulantly, she got out of the car and wiggled her bottom as she approached the policeman.

"What's she doing now?" asked the voice behind me.

"She's giving him two choices," I said.

We watched her stretch up to Newby's ear and whisper something that made his eyes sit up and beg. He handed her the Coca-Cola and, without looking back, marched to the junction, where he right-wheeled and disappeared.

Tucker and I climbed out of the car but, before he started across the road, I put a hand on his shoulder.

"I know what you're going to say, Mr Ned. The same as you told Sean on the record stall, years ago."

"You can turn around and walk away," I said. "You've not got too much dirt on your shoes."

He said that reporting the arrest of a murderer was too good an opportunity for an office junior to miss. He was right, of course. I said that most people walk through Goodladies Road and the spirit of the place doesn't touch them but it drags others down and they're never free of its sludge. It can take a proud man and break him. It can take an honest man and put a mirror at his face so that he doesn't know where to look. The folk who walked these pavements – the prostitutes and policemen, the mothers and fathers and owners of dogs – knew the ties that bound us all together. Each one had to invite their neighbours in for tea and never mind the mud on the carpet. But Kid Tucker, ace reporter, was only nineteen. How could he think of that day, when he was forty or fifty, when Goodladies Road might tap him on his shoulder and say 'Remember me?'

By the time we reached the pavement, Timbers had already knocked on Popinjay's door. "We're coming in," she said when he answered. She handed me the cola. I passed it to the boy.

"We're coming in, Pop," I confirmed.

"Arrest him, Edward."

We had been through this routine before. I put a hand on Popinjay's shoulder and said boldly, "Peregrine Popinjay, I'm arresting you for the wilful murder of Ronald Bulpit on or before ..."

"Before Sunday night. That's when he murdered Amy."

Tucker started to scribble in his notepad. "God, this is fantastic. The chief will think I'm marvellous." We were still standing on the doorstep. Popinjay hadn't said a word; he looked from one face to another.

"And for the murder of Amy Bulpit," I continued.

"And Boots Leonard," nodded Timbers.

"And the Bloated Boy?" I asked.

She said, "No, he's safe and sound by now and miles away. It's just the other three."

"You're arrested for the three of them." I turned to Timbers: "OK. Tell us how."

"You'd better come in," said Popinjay.

The room was bathed in yellow light, like dull English mustard, and a scent which should have conjured up Spring but, because of the cats, it smelled like cats. Pictures by Louis Wain, cut from old magazines and books, hung on every wall and stood on every table, and some old friends had come back from the taxidermist. There was something wrong about real cats sharing a room with stuffed ones but they seemed to get along. Four live ones filled his small front room, while Cinderella, the queen cat, sat proudly in the deck of an open gramophone. Popinjay left us. He went to the mirror in the hall and sang some nonsense to himself as he oiled his hair and dressed himself in his pearly smoking cap and jacket. When he came back, he clapped his hands. "I can offer green tea," he said but we all said no with one voice.

Timbers commenced her explanation. "At first, I thought it was Dr Debs. She told a lie at the hospital, you see. She said that she'd been called from the wards to see me, but other people mentioned that she hadn't been on duty at all. So, she could have done the murder and might have been trying to fool me with a false alibi. But I couldn't think of a connection between her and Amy Bulpit. Except the museum. The museum seemed to be the key. If she was a cleaner in the museum and Doctor Debs was on the hanging committee, well, there might be something there. But even when the tea ladies told me that she worked with them sometimes, I couldn't make anything of it. So, I had to find someone else who knew Amy in the museum." She said to Popinjay, "I didn't think of you. I simply didn't connect you – but why should you make things up about Ma, if you had nothing to hide?"

"Don't stand around like this," he said. "Why don't we all sit down?" But the cats had left us no chairs so we stayed on our feet and Popinjay didn't ask again. "I haven't made anything up," he argued quietly.

"And that's why you're guilty," she said. "Because you don't know the mistake that you made. It was Baby Tucker, here, who put me onto it. He and his Vicar's Locked Room Mystery. He said that it's a mistake to think you know who goes in and out unless you're watching the door all the time. Yet, you told Ned that Ma came back to the Cockleshells Club the second time carrying her cleaning gear. You couldn't have seen that, Mr Popinjay, because she didn't need to bring the gear with her. She'd left her brushes and buckets in the schoolhouse an hour before. So, if you weren't there, keeping watch, where were you?"

"Moving the body," I said, thinking aloud.

His stare was fixed, but his face twitched as the different ideas raced through his mind. I thought that he was going to offer another story. He picked up a cat, cradled it and fussed with its fur. Two more came and brushed against his legs. "There, there, kitties," he said softly. Then : "It was that picture of Widow McKinley that started it. I couldn't tolerate my lovely Tricorn being moved to make way for the old woman with her baked potatoes. I thought about wrapping the Tricorn in my overcoat and taking it home but I never thought I'd get away with it. Until I saw Mrs Bulpit cleaning after hours. I followed her home. I got to know her. I began to meet her, telephone her, interrupt her at work. Slowly she began to listen to me. I explained my plan to steal the picture but she was too scared to help me"

I put a hand to my forehead as the threads of the story came together. "At some point, Ron Bulpit must have caught a whisper of your ideas," I sighed, shaking my head. "Just a hint, but that was enough and the whole thing went awry. He passed the information but it got misinterpreted. 'Tricorn' was going to be stolen; not your bloody oil painting but the secret missile codes. Suddenly, poor old Ron became the main source in a spy investigation." I tried to laugh. "They established a special team with safe houses and listening posts."

"Fantastic," said Tucker, scribbling page after page. "Just fantastic."

"And which expert was going to say that the clues could be ignored? Yes, just as you say, Tucker – absolutely bloody fantastic."

"She was always saying that she couldn't stand her husband," Popinjay continued, fiddling with a loose pearl button on his fancy jacket. "So one day, when she wished that someone would kill him, I said yes. I'd get rid of her husband if she promised to help me remove HMS Tricorn."

"But she was horrified when you told her that you had murdered him," said Timbers.

"She threatened to go to the police."

"And you told her that you'd make sure the police would be able to prove that she did it."

"The silly, silly woman told you all about it. She must have known that I couldn't let her carry on like that. When I saw you run out of the school hall, I knew that she would be downstairs alone. You hadn't locked the doors, just banged them closed, and the cellar steps were bolted from the outside so it was easy. Mrs Bulpit knew that I'd come to kill her – she knew that she deserved it, she knew I had no choice. At first I was going to leave her there, dead on the floor but you came back, Miss Timber-Clever-Dick, and when you left with blood on your hands, I went back down to the cellar to see what you had done."

"Then young Boots turned up."

"He was struck dumb; he couldn't take it in. He was gibbering and shaking, taking nothing in. I told him that if he talked, I would blame him. I don't think he understood what I was saying so, piece by piece, I took his clothes and stuffed them about Mrs Bulpit's body. I put his underpants in her mouth, his socks between her legs; I tied his shirt sleeves around her neck and his trouser ..."

167

"Stop," I said. "We won't let you relive it. The woman is dead, for God's sake."

He laughed. "But you'll never find her body. Not for years and years!"

"When you threw him onto the street," Timbers said, "he was in no state to make any sense, so a cabbie picked him up, found him an old blanket and boots, and took him to the Royal Infirmary."

"But you had no reason to kill the Bloated Boy," I insisted angrily.

Timbers said quietly, "The Bloated Boy isn't dead. He saw what had happened to Boots and he was too scared to go out. Slowly looked after him through the week and Ma got him passage out of the city this morning."

"Good show," said Tucker. "If he gets the luck he deserves, he'll hear no more of this."

Popinjay offered his wrists for a pair of handcuffs. "I haven't got any," I said, shaking my head. "I should have suspected you when Doctor Deborah promised me that she wasn't outside the old schoolhouse. You couldn't have seen her because you weren't there."

"True, I wasn't there, but don't blame yourself, Machray. Why should you believe a woman who had already lied to you. After all, the lady is an exhibitionist, like the Popinjay himself – and you should never trust an exhibitionist."

"An exhibitionist?" queried Tucker.

Popinjay bent forward. "She shows off her feet to susceptible gentlemen." He checked his fob watch. "About now, if the CID have analysed the information I cooked up, they will be breaking up one of her parties. Dr Deborah and her fawns will be arrested but it should be only a few hours before the house of cards falls down and the detectives realise they've been fooled." He said very quietly to Tucker, "They'll be rather cross."

SIXTEEN

An Evening Walk

After the funeral, Herbert Jayne drove me to the foreshore. We parked on the scrub above the beach and talked about the Assitant Chief Constable for a few minutes. Then he said that he was going to take a look at Leonard's boat.

"I'll sit on my own, if you don't mind. Just for a while," I said.

I couldn't get it out of my head that, in some way, Adcum's suicide was my fault. He was isolated at work and ashamed of his friendship with Timberdick. Maybe he had brought out a dark side of his wife's nature; I didn't know that. But I had an uncanny certainty that, in the last seconds of his life, he was cursing Ned Machray.

Before I could lay these thoughts to rest, Herbie came running back up the beach, waving his hands and shouting. He had found Amy Bulpit's boodstained clothing.

Straightaway, I knew that Popinjay was playing with us. He knew that we would search the boat. He also knew that it would get us no nearer her body.

"Handle it, Herb," I said. "I've had enough."

"Sure, boy. Don't you worry."

I got out of the car.

"Can't you stand guard while I call Division?" he asked.

But I was already walking away.

I sat in the Volunteer until closing time, then dawdled through the alleyways to Goodladies Junction. It was a cool night with a cloudless sky, producing that freshness that goes with new beginnings and everything being all right. I stood at the crossroads with my raincoat unbuttoned and my hands loose in its pockets. I fancied that I looked like the logo on Hank Janson paperbacks but I knew other people would say I was too old and too fat.

I loved the place. The picture-houses had just turned out and the double-deckers were full. Our football team was doing well that season and a group of lads were hanging around the fish and chip shop, singing the anthems and waving a scarf. Two couples were kissing against the walls of the Hoboken Arms. Inside, the jukebox was playing the unexpired sequence of records, although the pub had emptied; sometimes the rock 'n' roll lasted for half an hour after the last drinkers left. Some of the naive and sentimental lyrics seemed like heavenly wallpaper for the kissing couples. Across the road, Mrs Thurrocks was sitting with her dog on the doorstep of Number 42; she would wait for the roads to clear before taking her last walk of the evening. The family in 42 were so used to people sitting on their doorstep that they continued their bedtime routine without speaking of the old woman and her dog.

Timberdick was standing on her 'little bit of pavement' opposite the Hoboken. I didn't walk across to her at once but watched her from the shadow of the pub's side gate. She was wearing her white shortie raincoat, of course, with little or nothing underneath, and the white high heels that were chipped and scratched. She'd had her hair cut recently, as short as a boy's. Her face looked well scrubbed, with a reddish blush to it. She was full of beans. She bobbed about, chuckling and giggling, even when no-one was there to listen. She'd found some of her old confidence, I decided.

"Did you look for me at the funeral?" she asked when I strolled up to her.

I shook my head.

"I didn't go because I thought I'd look wrong," she said.

"It was posh people and policemen who'd been to college. Adcum would have hated it."

"He had no choice, I suppose. I suppose he had to be there. What about her?"

"In the middle of it."

"I suppose she had no choice, just like him."

"But she didn't have to look like a cold-hearted cow," I said.

"It was my fault, wasn't it?" asked Timberdick. "What happened to them and how it all ended." She knew that the question was too complicated to answer. She allowed a decent pause, then asked, "Did you come here to see me?"

I shook my head again.

"I've just had a bloke in a dull green Popular," she said as if she were collecting points for an I-Spy book. "He wanted to show me his wife's invisible stitching on the passenger's side but the inside light's no good in old Fords. Are you sure you're not looking for me?"

She linked my arm and began to walk me down the side street. My hands were still in my coat pockets.

"Did you tell Len in the Volunteer that we'd take on that new case?"

"I told him to find a private detective."

"That's silly. We work well together, you and me. It would have been fun."

I knew that she was leading me to the Dirty Verger's old cottage.

"I want you to promise me."

I wasn't going to promise her anything, I said.

"Give up Slowly Barnes."

"I can't do that," I protested earnestly. "She comes round every Monday morning to play with my train set."

"I can do that. I can play trains."

"Not like Slowly, you can't."

She stopped us walking. We'd only got as far as Smee Ditchen's house – we still had twenty houses and two corners to go – but she'd decided to have it out with me. She turned to face me, went onto her toes and said, "Look. Look right at me. Now, stop sulking!"

I insisted I wasn't.

"You've been sulking for weeks, Ned Machray. It wasn't me who turned you down. It was Adcum Ops's fault. He said he'd throw you out of the Force if you married me. That's why I called it off and I was stupid. It was a stupid, stupid thing to do. It's what you want, isn't it? You want to be chucked out. Well, the soft bugger's gone now so there's nothing to stop us."

"Too late," I said, sulking more than ever. "Don't want to marry you anymore."

"But you must want me," she argued. "That's why you came to the junction tonight."

"I came," I said slowly and deliberately, "because I'm composing a talk for the All Women Modellers of Hazeley's Bottom."

"Poor Hazeley," she said, weakly repeating her old joke.

"I've been invited to speak and it helps to run it through my head when I'm walking."

"Go on, then."

"Go on then, what?"

She backed up against the brick wall and collected my fingertips in hers. "Run your talk through your head, but out loud because I'm here."

"I thought I'd start by introducing myself."

"Sounds good."

"My name is Ned Machray and I'm going to talk tonight about the principles of realistic compression."

"Sounds atomic. Let's practise."

THE TIMBERDICK MYSTERIES

"Noble has a fine knack of creating a sense of place and atmosphere. He has created an intriguing set of characters."

Portsmouth Post

"A marvellous creation. Noble reels off a first rate story. Vastly entertaining"

Nottingham Post

"He leaves you begging for the next in the series."

Montgomeryshire Advertiser

TIMBERDICK'S FIRST CASE
Matador Paperback
ISBN 1-904744-33-8

Timberdick worked the pavements of Goodladies Road where the men had bad ideas and the girls should have known better. In 1963, the murder of a prostitute challenges more than Timbers' detective skills. "Real people get murdered by their family and friends," says one of the girls. "We get killed by everyone else."

LIKING GOOD JAZZ
Matador Paperback
ISBN 1-904744-96-6

Searching for an abandoned infant, Timberdick learns that the father has been murdered. She can trust no-one, not even those who are close to her. Before it's all over, she's sure of only one thing. No place rocks like the Hoboken Arms on Tuesday night!

PIGGY TUCKER'S POISON
Matador Paperback
ISBN 1-904-905237-18-9

Timberdick is back! She's living in the vestry and working nights in the Curiosity Shop when a stranger is murdered at the top of the stairs. Timbers is arrested but she has no time to waste in a police cell. She has a murder to solve and a bun in the oven.

THE CASE OF THE DIRTY VERGER
Matador Paperback
ISBN 978-1905886-319

It's 1947 but there's still no peace of Goodladies Road. Men without a war and girls without homes is a cocktail for murder. We explore Timberdick's first nights on Goodladies Road and find clues to many of the characters that we have already met in her later cases.

THE PARISH OF FRAYED ENDS
Matador Paperback
ISBN: 978-1906221-799

When the Chief Constable asks questions about a superintendent who was buried two years ago, our street-wise detective finds that she is investigating three murders instead of one. But three suspects say that they were in bed with her favourite policeman on the night of the murder, so Timbers can see only one way forward. She sets a date for her wedding.

A MYSTERY OF CROSS WOMEN
Matador Paperback
ISBN 978-1848760-929

In 1937, Ned Machray has been a policeman for only a few weeks when he finds his first murder but, in this prelude to the Timberdick Mysteries, he solves the case that has baffled Scotland Yard, Whitehall and the local CID.

Keep up to date with Timberdick's website
www.bookcabin.co.uk